CHRI

13 MILES

NORTH

To Mary Lou

Thank you for your
purchase.

Enjoy

- Christina Lynne

13 MILES
NORTH

CHRISTINA LYNNE

Editor, Cover Artist Dixie Faughn II

Publisher Christina Lynne
2024

For rights and permissions, please contact:
Christina Lynne

darkhorse_20002000@yahoo.com

First Printing: 2024

ISBN 978-1-304-60518-4

Dedication

In memory of my best friend.
In large part, it is thanks to you that I discovered my
passion for writing.

I have felt your hand guiding me throughout the process
of creating this story.

Thank you for always being my partner in crime.

Thank you for the memories.
1981-2017

Contents

Acknowledgments

I want to thank my family and friends, especially my spouse and parents, who have encouraged me throughout this process, even helping me fight through writer's block.

Thank you for your kindness, patience, and many encouraging words. Special thanks to my high school English teacher, who was the first person to encourage me to get published.

Special thanks to those who have offered suggestions for making this dream come true!

Prologue

Solange: I still feel drawn to that piece of land all these years later. I suppose a part of me will always think of it as home. I feel conflicted when I do allow myself to think of it. It ended up costing me so much. Part of me wishes that I had never seen it. After all, if I had never laid eyes on it, it would have only existed in my dreams. I wouldn't be able to miss something I never had.

In the real world, it did exist. I lived there. I was married there. I made a life there and memories there with someone whom I loved. I made many memories there, good and bad. Eventually, the bad outweighed the good, and I left of my own free will.

It has changed hands now, and the property itself has changed. The once beautiful old red barn has begun to fade; its doors now sag, and its windows are all broken out. Overgrown grass and weeds have added to the look.

The house is now abandoned. The new owners have constructed a new modern-style structure and have chosen to live in it over the original house. The paint is slowly chipping from the trim that I once painted in the middle of winter. Once loved and well cared for, my flower beds are now overgrown with weeds. The old wooden screen door hangs on its hinges by a thread. The garage we worked so hard to build sits empty and unused. The new white siding we had installed is now slowly yellowing. The elements have now ravaged the shingles. The fruit trees I worked so hard to bring back have mostly been cut down or destroyed by nature.

Yet, it still calls to me to come home. That is the curse of 13 Mile Farm. I won't let it take me back. I have a new life now. I have moved on. To those who are there now, I wish you the best of luck. May that piece of land not be the death of your dreams as it was for me.

How We Started Out

Dakota and I had met when I was in my early twenties, and he was in his thirties. That was more of an age difference than with anyone I had dated previously. This, however, did not stop our romance.

There had been a steady stream of men in and out of my life as long as I had been allowed to date. All of them I had cared about, one of which I was sure I had very much loved. None of these relationships had a happy ending.

At the time we met, I was happily single. I enjoyed having fun with my friends and being a bit promiscuous. My best friend, Celeste, and I had gone in on a serious adult purchase together. We bought an older two-bedroom trailer house. We were both in need of some stability, as well as a place where we could still have fun.

Celeste was even more promiscuous than I was. She always had been. We had a lot of fun together. However, things had changed for her recently, forcing her to mature. She had a baby boy. Shortly afterward, she broke up with his father, Roman.

A few months after we bought the trailer, Roman had started coming back around. He just wouldn't leave her alone. Inevitably, she got back together with him and moved out, leaving me alone to deal with the trailer and the bills that went with it.

Life moved on. Friends visited. I worked. I paid the bills. Life was normal from the outside looking in. What no one noticed was that despite all the friends, the men in and out, and the continuous parties, I was lonely. Very lonely and entirely lost. I was getting to a point where all the guys surrounding me seemed more like boys. I just wanted to be loved. Loved unconditionally and permanently.

The days and the nights continued like this for two more years until one night completely changed my journey. I had been invited to a club with a friend, Tristan, and had gotten dressed up in a red party dress that stopped just above my knees. It hugged my ample curves nicely and showed off my long legs. I wore a pair of black wedge heels as an accent. My shoulder-length blonde hair was curled loosely and parted to one side. I wore eyeliner and dark gray eyeshadow to accent my gray-green eyes. I knew I looked good. I was on the prowl for someone to bring home.

It was the first weekend of legalized fireworks in our state. As we drove, we could see the beautiful bursts of multi-colored designs light up the sky. We had just gotten on the interstate heading south when a group of ambulances and firetrucks flew by, red and blue lights flashing and sirens blaring. They were heading north in the opposite lane. Tristan pulled over, and we looked back in the direction they had headed.

There was a large cloud of black smoke that looked like it was near my house! It was much darker and denser than the wisps of gray smoke we had frequently seen associated with the fireworks. I looked over at Tristan, a bit alarmed now. "That has to be a fire, and it looks close to my house. Do you think we should turn around and check?" I asked.

Tristan shrugged and said, "It's probably nothing. You're worrying too much."

We started back towards our destination. We drove a few more miles before I broke the silence. "I'm sorry. I really want to go home and check!" I looked at him with concern in my eyes. I had worked too hard for that little house to have something happen to it. If there were something I could do to protect it, I would. "We can still go to the club after we check to make sure everything is OK," I said. I kind of felt bad, but not bad enough to change my mind.

He looked disgusted. Tristan sighed and rolled his eyes at me. "Fine." We turned off at the next exit and headed back home.

The First Meeting

Solange: As we pulled up to the entrance of the trailer court, police vehicles blocked us from getting in. The smoke was thick now. My fears were confirmed. There was a fire in the trailer court! After a period of begging and telling the police officer that I lived in the court, they finally allowed us to enter.

The sight that met us was nothing less than terrifying. The trailer in the back of mine and the tree beside it were engulfed in flames. Several firefighters were behind my house, dousing the flaming trailer and tree with their hoses. I quickly entered my house to make sure everything was OK. My trailer was not on fire, Thank God! The rear bedroom where I slept was, however, very hot. I knew there was nothing I could do but wait. I grabbed my cat, put her in her carrier, and headed outside.

A large group had congregated outside in front of the next-door trailer to watch the firemen fight the blaze. I knew the trailer next door had recently changed hands, but I had yet to meet the new owner. Rumor had it that he was a police officer. I wondered if he was involved in responding to the fire.

As if someone had read my thoughts, the new neighbor walked out of his house, rubbing his eyes as if he had been asleep. He towered over almost everyone else in the crowd. He was broad across his shoulders, had the largest biceps I had ever seen, and had a defined chest that was obvious even through his shirt. He looked like he hadn't had a haircut in quite some time, and his shaggy, curly, sandy blonde hair was sticking up in all directions. I couldn't see his eyes through big square glasses. He was wearing gray sweatpants and what appeared to be a faded army-issued t-shirt. I was immediately attracted to him.

He stayed away from the rest of the crowd. I watched him walk over to one of the police officers who was blocking the crowd from getting too close to the fire and have a short conversation. He proceeded to walk back up to the front of his trailer, leaned against the front door, and watched the fire as it was slowly snuffed out. I thought I had seen him look my way once, but I couldn't be sure. He disappeared back into his trailer shortly after that point.

The fire was put out, and there was no damage to anything on my property other than some grass in my backyard, and one side of my tree's bark had been singed. Sadly, the trailer in the back of mine was a total loss. It hadn't burnt to the ground, but the center of it was charred on the outside, and the fire had burnt through the roof. What had been the tree next to it had no leaves left on it. It was diminished to a blackened stump with a few blackened limbs.

It was late by the time the excitement had ended. Tristan and I decided not to go out again that evening. Instead, we decided just to hang out at my place. As we sat on the couch having a drink, I asked Tristan if he had met the mystery man next door. He hadn't either. I was intrigued. I wanted to know more. I wanted to know the mystery man next door.

Getting to Know Each Other

Solange: Another couple of weeks went by without an event. I worked the day shift and rarely saw a vehicle next door. It was a hot mid-July afternoon. I didn't have any plans for the weekend, but I had a car show coming up on Sunday. Preparing the cars for the car show was always a long process, so I decided to get to work. My 69 Cutlass wouldn't take me long to get ready since it was still painted with primer, but my 84 Cutlass would take much longer.

I put on a pair of cut-off jean shorts and my bikini top. I grabbed my blue wash bucket and squeezed some of the pink car wash soap into it. I went over to my closet and grabbed my favorite soft cloth to wash with and another for drying. I also grabbed some degreaser, wheel polish, Wet Black, and interior cleaning spray. I grabbed some cotton swabs and my good wax. With a smile, I turned the cold and hot handles and watched the bucket fill with warm, sudsy water. I headed out the door to get to work. I loved washing my cars. They were my pride and joy.

I hooked the hose up to the waterspout on the front of my house and attached the spray nozzle to the hose. I turned on the spicket and started to spray down the exterior of the 69. The brownish water rolled off the black exterior in a satisfying way. Then, I started scrubbing the gray racing stripes lovingly and finally rinsed the entire car. When that was done, I moved on to drying each drop of water from my beautiful car.

Then, I moved on to cleaning under the hood. I sprayed degreaser over the chrome valve covers, hiding the raised red flames in white foam. I wiped them clean until I could see my own reflection in them. Lastly, I gave the interior one final inspection and moved on to wiping the rims and applying Wet Black to all four of the tires. I realized that it was getting dark. I was hot and sweaty. The 84 could wait until tomorrow.

I wiped the sweat from my forehead and turned away from the car. I turned, leaning against the car's fender, and found myself facing my next-door neighbor's house. As if appearing out of nowhere, there he was. He leaned lazily against his house with a crooked grin gracing his tanned face. He had gotten a haircut since I had seen him the first time, the night of the fire. He now sported a neatly trimmed goatee, which was darker than his hair. Previously hidden by a scruffy beard, I could now see that he had dimples. They added to his boyish good looks.

He wore a tan shirt similar to the one I had first seen him in and khaki pants. Again, I noticed his broad shoulders and the way that his biceps and chest bulged in the restrictive cap-sleeved shirt. I blushed a bit as we continued to study each other. His expression said that his thoughts at the sight of me were similar.

Dakota: I got off from work Friday evening after a long, hard shift. As I parked, the activity next door drew my attention. There she was. I remembered seeing her for the first time the night of the fire. I remembered admiring her as she stood next door, watching the trailer in the back of hers burn. She was all dressed up that night as if she had been going to a party. Damn, was she fine. She had long blonde hair, gray eyes, and legs up to her neck. I was immediately attracted to her.

I had not seen her since that night, and it seemed like we were on opposite shifts. There were always cars out front of her house. I wondered how many people lived there. More importantly, did she have a boyfriend?

To my pleasure, on this hot July evening, our paths appeared to be crossing again. I got out of my car and leaned against my trailer, hoping she would not notice me admiring her as she worked. She looked so enticing in a pair of cut-off shorts and a bikini top.

My heartbeat rapidly, about to jump out of my chest. She finished washing her car and turned my way. She looked me up and down as I studied her silently in turn. I hoped she didn't realize I had been standing there watching her and found it creepy.

Finally, I broke the silence. "Hey, I thought a guy lived here. There are always so many cars in and out of here, and the two cars and the pickup that are here all the time look like something a guy would drive." That seemed to get under her skin. Her expression turned to a frown. I didn't seem to be making a good impression. Oh shit! I had put my foot in my mouth with that statement.

Her hands went to her hips. "No, those are mine," she said. Her annoyance was coming through in her voice as well as in her body language.

"Whoa, I didn't mean to offend you," I apologized. My hands rose up in front of my face as if I could stop her anger. Now, she seemed amused by my concern. I felt like she was sending me mixed signals!

She cracked a smile and let her arms fall back to a relaxed position. Despite the mixed signals, I found myself starting to like this beautiful stranger. "Let's start over. My name is Dakota. What's yours?" I asked with what I hoped for was a winning smile.

"My name is Solange. Nice to meet you, Dakota." We stood in her yard, talking about her cars and the upcoming car show. Finally, she asked, "Would you like to hang out?" returning my smile. I cautiously accepted. We headed to her backyard.

Though we lived in a trailer court, her lot had a fair-sized yard, a couple of lawn chairs, and a table in the backyard. She even had a small garden. The remnants of the fire were still noticeable, though her yard was well-kept. The yard was neatly mowed and had some flowers in an old pot on the small table. She seemed to be very proud of having a place she owned at a young age.

We lost track of time and ended up talking late into the night. As we got to know each other, I revealed that I had just finished several years in the military. I told her that I had served in the Army but found that it no longer interested me and decided to get out instead of making a career of it.

I elaborated, explaining that I had served eight years on active duty and just finished another four years as a reserve. I joined in my early twenties. I worked various short-term jobs without any real direction after graduating high school. Looking for that direction, I joined the military.

Now that I was out permanently, I work at the county jail. I explained that I was enjoying it so far, and it was forcing me to stay in shape. She must have thought that was obvious. I smiled as I watched her admire my chest and arms. I knew that I looked much younger than my actual age. She looked at me doubtfully as I continued telling her about my past.

"Show me your driver's license. There is no way you are old enough to have done all of that," she stated.

"I told you how old I am. Don't you believe me?" I asked.

"No, I don't," she smirked. "Now, hand it over."

I pulled my license out of my wallet and handed it to her. I was concerned that the night may be over when she saw my date of birth. Her face said it all. I was in my thirties. Several years older than her. Her disappointment was evident. I wondered if she had been hoping that I hadn't told her the truth about my age. The look on her face stung my pride.

"Well, I guess I should be leaving," I stated as I stood up to return to my house. I figured any chance I had was now blown with her due to our age difference. I saw her face redden a bit. I didn't know exactly how to react.

Solange: I couldn't believe that he was actually as old as he had told me. I had really hoped that my estimation of his age would be close, but now I knew it was not. I liked him. I could tell that he liked me too. The logical part of us was saying that what the physical part of us wanted was a bad idea. "Friends?" I asked. I looked up from his license, smiled, and handed it back to him.

He sat back down but seemed a bit uncomfortable. We talked a bit more. I found out that he was an only child, and his family lived on the other side of the state. He settled here due to his reserve unit being based here. I couldn't put my finger on it, but he seemed guarded. Despite that and my concerns about the age difference, the draw I felt towards him was undeniable.

I told him that I was the oldest of two girls and that my parents were divorced, but both lived nearby. My mom, Charlotte, married Waylon, and my dad, Leonard, married Karen.

I also told him about the still painful breakup I had gone through about a year previously. As I shared, he seemed a bit more comfortable but did not share any further information about himself.

Things Began to Get Serious

Solange: After that evening, Dakota and I started to hang out regularly. Being next-door neighbors, it was easy to see each other whenever we wanted to, when our schedules allowed. We spent as much time together as we could, and we became pretty inseparable.

Several months after our initial visit, I came home, and Dakota was sitting on the front deck of my trailer waiting for me. He smiled as I approached. "Hey, we didn't have plans tonight, did we?" I asked.

"Nope. I wanted to surprise you," he said.

"Ok, well, consider me surprised. Come on in. It's cold out here," I said. By this time of the year, the snow hadn't fallen yet, but you could tell by the cold, crisp air that it could happen any day. We entered the warm house, and Dakota plunked down on my old couch, patting the seat next to him expectantly.

I sat down next to him and gave him a strange look. He appeared to be a bit nervous. I found his demeanor odd as we had become close friends, and there wasn't much we wouldn't say to or do around each other. I knew something had to be up. "OK, what's up? You're acting really weird, Dakota," I said. He gave me a nervous smile. "Just say what's on your mind. You're weirding me out," I said, now slightly concerned.

He looked me in the eyes. "Well, I have been struggling with just being your friend for a while..." Dakota's words trailed off as he looked at me for a reaction.

I just stared at him blankly. He had just voiced exactly what I had been feeling, but I refused to admit it. My heart burst with affection. I smiled, scooted a fraction closer, and grabbed his face with both hands. I placed a careful kiss on his lips. His eyes went wide.

"Well, I guess that means I can consider you my girlfriend?" Dakota asked.

I nodded my head in reply. At that moment, nothing could have made me happier. After we were officially together, things moved quickly. We had already spent a lot of time together when we were friends. That now extended into spending nights together between our houses as often as possible. We spent a lot of time just lying around the house and talking.

We still hosted parties in our backyards. He came to my car shows with me, though he wasn't really into cars. He met my family and started hanging out with my friends. I also met his family and hung out with his friends. We found out about each other's hobbies and learned to enjoy them together. One of our mutual favorites turned out to be karaoke. We enjoyed hanging out in our love bubble, alone, mostly. We went on dates and slowly got to know each other even better.

After about a year and a half of dating, Dakota asked me to go out with him for my birthday. He had invited a group of our closest friends and even rented a limo for us to arrive in. We would drive around town as a group for a bit, then go to supper and karaoke at our favorite spot. He had even rented us a room for the evening.

We all piled into the limo, enjoyed peeking our heads out the moon roof, and drinking from the mini-bar. Our large table ordered pizza and barbequed wings at the bar. We sat, enjoying the others singing, and then it was Dakota's turn to sing.

Dakota got up on stage and sang his favorite Elvis song, a perfect rendition in my eyes. He looked at me as he sang as if singing a love song directly to me. In the end, instead of handing the microphone back to the DJ, he kept it and began to speak. My heart stopped. My hand went to my mouth. *What was he doing?*

"Sorry to interrupt the program, folks, but I have something I need to do. Solange, will you come up here, please?"

I froze in my seat as the stage spotlight was pointed at me. I was caught totally off guard. I slowly stood up and joined him on the stage. I felt like there were butterflies in my stomach.

"Solange, this past year and a half has been the happiest of my life, thanks to you coming into it. You have filled a void in my life that I didn't even know was there. Would you do me the honor of being my wife?"

I was speechless. My eyes filled with tears. I shook my head as I accepted. He handed the microphone back to the DJ, and we kissed our first kiss as an engaged couple on stage in that spotlight.

I snapped out of shock quickly. I was already on the stage and had put in a song to sing earlier in the evening. I asked the DJ to switch the song I had originally requested to sing to 'our' song and allow me to sing next. He gladly complied, and I belted it out as I had many times before, now with more meaning. There I was, standing in front of a bar full of strangers and a few of our friends, overjoyed that he had just asked me to marry him. I was over the moon with joy. I felt so lucky to have this handsome man who loved me as much as I loved him.

Planning the Wedding

Solange: Dakota sold his trailer and moved in with me. We continued our lives, good and bad, together. We very much enjoyed this time in our lives. Together, we began to plan our wedding but ran into a roadblock while we were looking for a place we could agree on to hold the wedding and reception.

I was a country girl and had my heart set on a country wedding in or near an old barn. The setting didn't matter as much to him as long as we got married and had our friends and family present. The problem we ran into was that all the locations we liked were booked for any of the summer dates we were considering. Our dream was to have a summer or early fall wedding. We had also decided to look for a place together instead of staying in my trailer house. We had looked at several places in town, but nothing seemed to fit our taste.

One night, after work, Dakota came home with excitement written all over his face. "I've got a surprise for you!" he said and proceeded to usher me out to his car. Dakota was very secretive about where we were going. It was already dark, so I was confused as to what the surprise could be. "It will only take about twenty minutes to get to where we are going." He told me enthusiastically.

I was amused at his enthusiasm and decided to let it be a surprise since he seemed very excited. We drove in silence out of town and into the countryside. There were no turns on our route other than the turn onto the old highway, which led out of town.

Enter 13 Mile Farm

Dakota: As I had promised, we drove about twenty minutes, then pulled over to the side of the road across from an acreage. I looked over at Solange and smiled. "This just came on the market today. I thought you might like it when I saw the pictures. It's a total of ten acres. It includes a house, a barn, and a couple of old buildings someone could either try to save or tear down. The best part is, it's in our budget!" The words spilled out of my mouth rapid fire. My eyes sparkled with excitement.

Solange seemed equally as excited, although all we could really see of the place was the profile of the buildings and trees, as the only light was from the moon and the headlights of the car. I was captivated. I felt a draw to the place and a bit of an attachment already.

Solange smiled back at me. "OK, let's take a look at it during the day and make a decision from there."

We drove past the place, turned around, and went past it again before heading home. The next day, we made an appointment with the realtor. We were scheduled to look at the place during the day on the upcoming Saturday when we would both be off from work.

We met the realtor, a young, well-dressed man, at 13 Mile Farm. He seemed nervous and talked too much, in my opinion. He was quick to inform us that there were several interested parties, though the place had only been on the market for a few days. He explained that the place was priced below its actual value due to the current owners wanting to sell it quickly—something about a divorce.

Solange: We first walked up to the house. In the daylight, we could see that the house was good sized. It was a two-story white house with gray trim. There was a sidewalk leading from the driveway to a brick patio with a wooden fence on one side and a planter full of dirt against the side of the house. It had a storm door that looked like an old wrought iron gate in front of a glass door. There was a heavy old wooden door behind the storm door whose age glaringly contrasted with the storm door.

We entered the house. The first room was an unfinished mudroom with a wooden bench to sit on and a coat rack. We took off our shoes and hung up our coats. The mud room led into the kitchen. There was also a steep set of stairs leading down to the basement. The kitchen was large but badly in need of an update. The wallpaper was peeling, the appliances old and dated, the cupboards painted white with many thick coats of paint, and the floors sported very worn brown patterned linoleum. The light in the center of the ceiling flickered slightly as the realtor hit the switch. The house mostly smelled of cinnamon, but the old house smell was still present.

The house also had a large living room and dining room. The floors were the original hardwood, and each room included what looked to be original woodwork with tall ceilings. The main level also featured a den and a small half bath. The living and dining rooms had large picture windows with stained glass accents. I assumed their view would be to the backyard.

I was pleasantly surprised when I looked out of the dining room window and discovered a four-season porch! The dining room also had a large bay window looking out towards the tree grove. Behind another heavy wooden door were two sets of creaky steps with a landing between them leading to the upper level.

The upper level had two large bedrooms and a smaller one. Both larger bedrooms had walk-in closets. One bedroom was partially wallpapered and painted light blue with a light blue carpet. The other larger one was painted pink. The smaller bedroom was white and had race car trim as if it were a child's room. The original hardwood was visible where there was no carpeting.

The thing that drew my attention and made me feel slightly uncomfortable at the same time was the hallway between the rooms. It seemed to go on forever, though I knew it had to be just an optical illusion.

"Hallway from hell," I muttered, chuckling to no one in particular. I smiled over at Dakota. I really liked the house and thought that it had great bones. I was already making plans for changes we could make secretly in my head.

After thoroughly exploring the house, we bundled back up and headed back outside to look at the rest of the property and the outbuildings. There were several buildings in varying states of disrepair. The two that I thought would be easiest to save were a pole shed that would be perfect for a garage and a large old barn that was just begging to be explored.

As we walked around, the realtor told us about the property. It was originally purchased in 1925 by a young couple, Cecil and Matilda Amos. Cecil came from a wealthy family on the east coast. While on a business trip to the Midwest, he met Matilda, a young farmer's daughter who would later become his wife. They had gotten the land as a gift from his parents for their wedding. The house and barn had gone up in 1926.

Cecil and Matilda had farmed the land and even had a small fruit orchard. Some of the fruit trees were still present on the acreage, though their age was showing. All of this further piqued my interest in the place.

As we entered the barn, I felt goosebumps form on my arms and butterflies in my stomach. The same odd, uncomfortable feeling I had felt earlier in the hallway upstairs in the house. Only stronger. The paint on the barn was faded and peeling. It appeared more pink than red. Some of the windows were broken out. The appearance of the roof clashed with the appearance of the rest of the barn. It was roofed with black tin. I suspected that is why the barn had held up so much better than the other buildings. The realtor opened a large sliding door. The sun hit the dust that had been stirred up, giving the barn's interior an eerie, smokey look. The realtor flipped the light switch, causing the illusion to fade.

I coughed a bit as we entered the lean-to portion of the barn. The lean-to was open, with a concrete floor. There was a door the size of a standard entry door but split into two sections leading into the main portion of the barn to our right. I walked towards the entry door ahead of the rest of the group.

The realtor was still rambling to Dakota about the selling points of the farm. In order to get into the next room, I had to open both sections of the door. I swung it open and stepped up into the main portion of the barn. The main portion of the barn appeared to be split up into three sections. The sections were separated by a half wall. It looked like there should have been gates running vertically to make the room have two large stalls and a large open area. Nothing remained of the gates but some rusty latches now. I stopped my exploration momentarily and allowed my mind to wonder what kind of animals had once occupied these stalls. Could it have been horses? A milk cow or two? Maybe even goats? The original owners must have had animals to provide them with food, as well as the crops they raised.

The third section, a smaller room with its own door, had a hydrant and a couple of shelves built into the walls, nothing else. I imagined turning this room into a tack room and filling it with equipment for my horses as well as storing their feed in there.

There was a set of steps that appeared to lead up to a hay loft. As I left the small room and headed towards the stairs to the loft, the goosebumps and butterflies returned. This time, they were accompanied by a lightheaded feeling and a slight headache. *What was going on? Was this all in my head?* I headed up the wooden stairs cautiously. The stairs appeared to be rickety, but they were surprisingly sturdy and had no trouble supporting my weight. Once again, the dust stirred around me. It must have been a while since anyone had been up there.

Finally, the realtor and Dakota caught up to me. "Do you hear that?" I asked Dakota as we ascended the stairs.

"What"? He responded.

"Never mind," I said. *I must be hearing things,* I thought to myself. Up until that point, I had almost forgotten that there were others with me. Again, I thought

I heard something. Was that.... piano music? I shook my head just a bit and blew it off as a figment of my imagination. I started to feel fainter as we neared the top of the steps. I knew I had allergies, so I figured that all the symptoms I had started to experience must have been related.

As I hit the top step, time seemed to slow almost to a halt. It was as if the others behind me, including the busily chattering real estate agent, ceased to exist. I stepped into the hayloft. Amidst old straw and a few discarded farm tools stood a player piano! Directly above the piano was the rusty, bent rim of a basket-ball hoop. Below it, on the floor, lay a flat, very old basketball.

I could see the discolored keys of the piano slowly begin moving on their own. The same off-key, eerie melody I had thought I heard before seemed to be coming from the piano as the sheet that contained the music slowly rolled inside the mysterious instrument. Though the keys moved and the sheet music rolled inside the piano, the grime on the worn keys appeared to remain unaltered.

A hand placed gently on my shoulder snapped me back to reality. "Hey, can I get a look up there?" Dakota asked.

I quickly made my way further into the loft, allowing the others to enter behind me. As I looked at Dakota, I could see concern in his eyes. I had hoped no one had noticed my brief exit from reality, but clearly, he had. "What? My allergies made me hesitate to go up there with all that old dirty stuff." I added a fake cough for effect. He shrugged and wandered around in the loft.

"Be careful; I don't know how the floors are in here with the age of this building," the realtor squeaked nervously.

I noticed that he was still standing at the entrance of the loft. *He probably doesn't want to get his fancy clothes dirty or scuff his pretty shoes,* I thought to myself as I rolled my eyes.

"Seems pretty solid to me," Dakota piped up as he bounced up and down on the floor for effect. He headed towards the piano. "Cool! Look at this neat old stuff!" he said as he veered towards the basketball next to the piano. He picked it up and lofted it at the rusty, bent hoop. He missed by a mile. The ball hit the wall of the barn near the large drop-down door with a thud. The ball rolled into the straw with the flat spot from the wall up. Dakota looked at me, and we both giggled. Next, he sauntered over to the piano. My smile quickly faded as a feeling I could only describe as dread overtook me. He hit a key, and an awful off-keynote rang out.

For a moment, I was sure it was not Dakota I saw standing in front of the piano, but instead, a man of a much smaller, thinner build. He wore a button-down, long-sleeved shirt, old-fashioned trousers, heavy work boots, and dark, slicked-back hair. Suspenders held up the trousers, which appeared too large for him. The unfamiliar man turned to look at me. The face I saw was definitely not Dakota's! His face appeared wrinkled and gaunt as he scowled at me. I gasped and took a staggering step backward, falling into the moldy old straw and immediately starting to cough. Dakota rushed to my side. The realtor scampered over as well, looking like he wanted to be anywhere but where he was. The two of them quickly helped me to my feet.

"What was that?!" Dakota questioned me with concern.

I was embarrassed by my fall and uncertain of what I just saw or why no one else seemed to be seeing the same thing. I knew I couldn't tell the truth as to what was actually going on. "The dust and moldy old straw in here are killing my allergies!" I said, trying to sound sincere. "Do you think we could get out of here and see the rest of this place?" I asked the realtor. He happily obliged and hurried us down the stairs and out of the barn.

The rest of the tour went on without event other than the occasional concerned glance from Dakota. Whenever I caught him looking my way, I shot a glare or an eye roll back at him. The symptoms I had been feeling lessened the further we got from the barn, and the incident was not brought up again.

Upon closer inspection of the other outbuildings, we determined that they were in much worse shape than we had assumed. I thought to myself that they would likely have to be demolished with the exception of one small shed, the pole shed we planned to use as a garage, and the barn.

As we returned to the front of the property, what the realtor was saying began to pique my interest again. On the opposite side of the driveway from the house was the remainder of the orchard that I had seen from the living room of the house. "I know they don't look like much now since they aren't in bloom, but when spring comes, they will," he beamed as he gestured to the tree line with his hand.

There was the sick feeling beginning to creep back again. This time, my chest tightened a bit, and my throat felt dry. *This has got to be allergies,* I thought to myself. Allergies did not explain what I had thought I saw and heard in the barn. I hoped no one else noticed as I cleared my throat as quietly as possible.

"Those fruit trees were part of the orchard that this property's original owners planted here as part of their farming operation in the late 1920s to early 1930s." He continued to rattle on, but a particular tree had caught my attention.

It was the largest of the trees and appeared to be constructed from several trees that had twisted together and grown into one very large, interesting tree.

As I looked, I thought I saw some movement near it. I cocked my head and squinted. The sick feeling once again got stronger. I thought I saw a thin woman in a dress peek out from behind the large, gnarled tree. I blinked rapidly. After I blinked, whatever I thought I saw was gone. I turned my attention back to the rambling realtor. Luckily, no one had noticed my attention being drawn elsewhere this time. He gestured with his hands again.

"The largest tree is a pear tree or rather several pear trees that grew into one. From stories I have heard, that one was the favorite of Matilda Amos. She planted it and cared for it with her own hands. It is the first to flower in the spring, and the pears are ripe and sweet after the first frost. I have heard they make excellent jam," he finished.

My eyes grew wide, recalling what I thought I had just seen. *Could I have just seen Matilda?*

"And that's about it," he concluded, drawing my attention back to the present. "What do you two think?"

"We will talk it over and get back to you by the end of the business day tomorrow," Dakota replied.

Moving to 13 Mile Farm

Solange: The next day, I contemplated what to do. An anxious feeling sat in my stomach as I remembered the strange happenings and the sick feeling I had experienced at the farm the day before. I could see the farm as a wonderful place to build a home with the love of my life. I decided that the good outweighed the bad and made my announcement to Dakota.

Dakota made the call. "I think we found a place for our wedding to happen and our new home!" He excitedly announced to the realtor. I pasted a smile on my face, hoping we had made the right decision. We signed the paperwork shortly thereafter and moved in during the first month of winter. We were fortunate and avoided all but a light snowfall. Family and friends helped us move our belongings in and arrange our new house into a home. We moved my grandpa's old pool table into the den along with my fiancé's military memorabilia, some of my collectibles, my dart board, and my car show trophies. Grandma's hutch and all its treasures went into the dining room.

We planned that once we were able to start remodeling, the upstairs bathroom and the kitchen would need to be remodeled first. Since we had a wedding to plan and pay for, anything other than paint would have to wait for the time being. Now that the house felt like home, the outside needed to be addressed.

We knew we wanted to have our wedding in front of the barn and the dance and reception in the hay loft, but the wedding wasn't set to happen until late the following summer. More importantly, we needed to repair the stalls in the barn so that we could bring the horses home from my dad's. We couldn't put up permanent fencing around the pasture until after spring thaw, so the stalls would need to be functional. Some square tubing fence would have to be put up so they could be outside until then.

We purchased an old M Farmall tractor from my dad, Leonard to move snow and bales, along with enough round bales to get the horses through winter. At least that was taken care of. My dad had promised to come help with the construction of doors for the stalls, as well as getting the temporary winter horse pen constructed. He also assured me that he and his wife, Karen would assist with tearing down the old weave fencing and posts and getting the new permanent fencing put up once spring allowed it.

It only took a week of work to get the lower level of the barn fit for the horses and their pen completed. Then my dad brought my black mare, Rampage, and her bay yearling son, Tornado, out to what was to be their new home. As he approached, I could hear my mare nervously pawing at the trailer floor. Her son let out an excited nicker as Dad backed up to the small barn door leading to the stalls. My horse had always hated being trailered.

I waved excitedly at my dad as he shut off the engine of his old Chevy truck. This was the first time I had been able to have my horses since I had moved away from Dad's acreage. He had been kind enough to keep them for me for the last several years. Dad unfolded his 6'6" frame out of the pickup and greeted me with a hug and smile. "I hope she didn't give you too much trouble loading," I snickered.

"Oh, you know how she is." He drew out each word as if to emphasize them.

"Let's get her out of here before she hurts herself," I said with concern. I could hear her pawing and snorting as I approached. "Hey Girl, it's me." She calmed some at the sound of my voice.

I opened the back doors of the trailer and continued to speak to her as I patted her hindquarters. I felt her body shiver a little as I worked my way up to her head. She let out a soft nicker as I untied her lead rope and backed her out of the trailer. Dad followed with Tornado. I buried my head in her mane and took in the wonderful aroma only a horse can produce.

Dakota stood by the larger barn door, watching cautiously. This was his first experience with horses or, really, any rural life. As I led Rampage closer to the barn, she began to prance and pull away from me. I thought maybe it was a reaction to her new surroundings. "Easy girl, easy," I repeated as I tried to pat her neck and lead her nearer to the barn door.

Suddenly, she reared, knocking me to the ground and pulling the lead out of my hands. I fell hard on my back, knocking all the wind out of me. I winced in pain, trying to catch my breath. I tried to stand up to get control of my horse. As I did, the pain caused the world to go dark briefly. As I blinked, I saw the same man I had previously seen in the hayloft, in old-fashioned clothing, standing beside the barn door, snickering with what looked to be a sneer on his face. I took a deep breath, finally able to force air back into my lungs. I blinked rapidly, and he was gone.

My dad had a hold of Rampage, and she appeared to be calming some. Dakota was behind me, holding Tornado and trying to coax me to stand up. I shook my head and groaned as I picked myself up off the ground. "Uh, oh, someone hasn't been around her horse much lately," my dad teased. Everyone seemed to find me getting knocked on my butt amusing now that the horses were under control, and I was OK.

I grabbed the lead from my dad as I rolled my eyes at him. "OK, let's try this again, you stubborn old nag!" I said to Rampage, only half joking. Her eyes almost looked like she was sorry. This time, she walked through the door without incident. *What in the world is going on...* I wondered. I knew what I had seen, but yet again, no one - other than my horse - seemed to have witnessed the old man sneering at me. Dad led Tornado into the stall, and both horses were calm.

Moving Towards the Wedding

Solange: After the incident with Rampage, everything seemed to go normal for quite some time. We painted the living room and dining room. The living room went from having wallpaper to having tan walls that accented the soft red carpet. The dining room gained red walls with tan accents to match the living room. I lined the bay window in the dining room with plants, placed red cushions in the sitting area, and added sheer red curtains.

Dakota rented a buffer and buffed the old wood floors to a shine. After painting it a dark blue with a gray ceiling, we put up some shelves in our bedroom and set up all my vintage gaming consoles. The house was really turning into our dream home. The only downside was that we were both exhausted between working full-time and working on our new home. As this continued, we both began to become increasingly irritable.

As the months progressed, we entered into premarital counseling with the pastor who was to be officiating our wedding. The first few sessions went relatively well; however, I could feel Dakota's resentment and annoyance building as the questions got more personal.

We were working on cleaning the old straw out of the hayloft for the upcoming wedding quite a bit during the week after work. It was a lot of work and dust, which aggravated my allergies and left me tired and cranky most evenings. Dakota had switched from night to day shift at his job, which he had not adjusted well to. Between working our jobs, farm work, and wedding planning, we were both exhausted. Though we still enjoyed our time together, it felt like our love bubble was beginning to shrink and feel cramped.

One particular evening, before cleaning up for pre-marital counseling, the inevitable happened. We had just finished pitching the last bit of straw out of the large door of the hay loft. I smiled as the last large bundle drifted from my pitchfork down to the waiting pickup bed. "Finally done. All that's left now is to sweep up here, and it's ready!" I wiggled my nose as a sneeze threatened to escape.

We placed our pitchforks against the wall, raised the door, and embraced each other in a joyful hug. We headed to the house with just enough time to get showered and dressed before counseling. I busied myself gathering ingredients for supper as Dakota prepared to shower.

As he slid off his shirt, he noticed that the silver chain, which usually held the large Sterling Silver ring that had belonged to my grandfather, was missing. I had given him the ring that meant so much to me when we had gotten engaged. It had been too large for me, so I had put it on the chain. It was also too large for Dakota's hand, so he had always worn it on

the silver chain as well. As I never removed my en-
gagement ring, he never removed the chain. He
slowly came out of the bathroom, shirtless. I could see
something was wrong through his body language. He
looked... guilty. I spoke before he did. "What's
wrong?"

"I think I lost your grandpa's ring," he said, droop-
ing his head in shame.

"What?!?!" I immediately stopped preparing our
meal. My hands dropped to my hips, and my eyes nar-
rowed.

"I think it fell off while we were cleaning out the hay
loft. I took off my shirt, and it wasn't there," Dakota explained.

"Did you take it off somewhere?" I asked, my temper flaring quickly. Between exhaustion from the work
on the barn, my job, and stress, my emotions were already running high. The loss of the precious hand me
down from my grandfather pushed me over the edge.

"No, it never leaves my body," he said.

I took a deep breath and tried to calm myself. "OK,
here's what we are going to do. We are going to tear
apart every square inch of the house, and if we still
don't find it, we will search through all the straw in that
truck bed!"

He looked confused, angry, and guilty all at once. "What about counseling?" He asked.

I was no longer able to hold my temper. "Screw it! This is more important! I will call the pastor now to re-schedule!" I screamed.

After searching the house and unloading all the straw onto the ground, sifting through it, and then re-loading it back into the truck bed, the chain and ring were not found. I fell to the ground, exhausted, dirty, and defeated. I laid my face in my hands and started to sob in anger and sadness.

"That ring was one of the last things I had left of Grandpa! I gave it to you to show you how much you mean to me, and I thought you would take care of it!" Now, I was screaming at him. He came to my side quickly and laid his hand on my shoulder. "Don't frig-gin touch me!" I yelled. I stood up and looked him squarely in the eye. "I'm taking my cat, some clothes, and going to Mom's! Show up at the church tomorrow, and I might too. Otherwise, you can explain to the pastor what happened!" His mouth opened as if to say something. "Don't! Trust me, we are both better off if I am not here tonight!" I knew he had never seen me so mad before. I was so exhausted and angry. I knew I was in the wrong for being so angry for something out of his control, but it didn't matter to me. The logical part of my brain had stopped working.

There was not another word spoken that night. I did exactly what I said: packed my cat in her carrier, grabbed some clothes, and headed for my mom's in my Cutlass. Little did I know that this would be the first of four times I would leave Dakota before it all came to an end.

The following day, I showed up at the church for counseling. I could see Dakota leaning against his small sedan, waiting to see if I would show up or not. I pulled the Cutlass up next to him and schooled my face to be blank as I turned the car off and got out.

Again, I spoke before he could. I held my hand up in front of me to imply that I wanted no comment from him. "Let's just get through this, and we will talk about it when we get home." The tension between us made the air feel thick.

"OK," was the only response I received. We walked to the church office side by side, but not hand in hand. The pastor looked up from his desk, where he had been reading through what I assumed to be notes from our previous sessions, and smiled. His smile quickly faded as he observed our body language. He greeted each of us with a warm handshake as we took our seats across the desk from him. As each session before had started, he asked us how things had been going since the last session.

This time, I let Dakota lead. I looked over at him to see what his reaction would be. He looked down at his feet, then shot the pastor a convincing smile. "Great! We finished cleaning the loft out for the wedding yesterday." I saw his hand absentmindedly toy with his shirt collar where the chain and ring usually sat.

My eyes shot downward, knowing we had agreed not to talk about it. It was becoming increasingly more difficult, with the pastor's gaze shifting between us. I knew that the pastor could tell something was wrong. He had been my pastor for many years. He had even baptized me. He knew me well. Despite my lack of comment so far into the session, he could see that there was an issue between the two of us. He continued with the session, starting with a discussion comparing the answers to a questionnaire we had each filled out individually and privately.

As he read our responses, it surprised me that our answers were so different. Up until now, our views had seemed to align. My face said it all when the question about children was answered. I did not want any, but he wanted three. I had assumed that at his age, his answer would have been the same as mine! At that point, I couldn't hold my tongue any longer. "What is that all about? I thought you didn't want any kids?" I questioned.

His face went red. "You never asked." His head was down, and his response was almost inaudible as it was so quiet.

The pastor chimed in at that point. "What is going on with you two today? Something has been off since you got here. What are you hiding?"

"Nothing," Dakota stated shortly.

I had reigned in my emotions long enough. I was unable to hold in the anger that had been festering since last night. "Let's just get it over with," I said. "He lost my grandpa's ring." My eyes swam with tears that I refused to let flow before the pastor.

Dakota raised his voice, the first time I remembered him doing so. "Damn! It's not like I meant to! I have not taken it off since you gave it to me!"

I looked at him with a challenge in my eyes. "It doesn't matter! If you can't even take care of a ring, what makes you think you could do any better with these three kids that you want?!"

I hadn't noticed the pastor watching the escalating fight with concern. He stood up, moved around his desk, and got between us.

"I have heard enough! It has become clear through the last several sessions, and especially today. Between what has just happened and your answers to the questionnaires, I cannot, in good conscience, proceed to marry the two of you! Please leave my office."

We looked at each other and then at the pastor. It was clear that he meant what he said. I went from being angry at Dakota to being embarrassed and dumbfounded. Now, what were we going to do?

We did as the pastor instructed. We made our way out to the parking lot quietly. Once there, I couldn't hold back the tears anymore. The sadness and concern outweighed my anger towards Dakota. I turned to him. "Our first real fight, and we screwed everything up. What are we going to do now?" I asked.

He wrapped me in his large arms and put his chin atop my head. "It's just a roadblock, dear. We have a lot to work on, but I'm willing if you are." His demeanor was now back to being calm, as if nothing had ever happened.

It had been an exhausting couple of days. We went directly to bed when we got home. I slept fitfully. Sometime during the night, I began to dream. It was like no dream I had ever had before. It felt like I was awake. I could see myself standing in the hayloft as if I were watching a movie, and I was the star. As I watched myself standing there, the man dressed in his olden-days clothes appeared as if out of nowhere. His form wasn't quite as solid as a human should be. I saw myself jump back as he approached. His mouth began to move as he neared, as if he had something to say.

As quickly as the man appeared, the woman in her old-time dress appeared, blocking his way to me. He snarled at her as she looked over at me. Her face seemed sad. "It's only just begun," said the old woman. I barely heard the words. I bolted upright in bed, gasping for air. *It had only been a dream, right?*

Trying to Move Past the Hurdle

Solange: After we lost our pastor, we knew we would need to find someone new to perform our wedding. We also agreed that we needed to finish our counseling. There were issues that we needed some professional help working through.

Several months later, it was time for the wedding. We had finished counseling, and things seemed to be going much smoother. There had been a few times we had argued, but nothing like before.

It was a warm, cloudless day. Family and friends were seated on both sides of a white runner leading from near the house to the front of the newly painted barn. Julius, the first friend I made when my family and I moved to the town where I grew up, sat at a DJ station inside the large barn door, playing some of our favorite music before the ceremony.

The horses stood beside the barn as if waiting. Celeste, my oldest friend; Daisy, the Third Musketeer from our high school group; Sky, who had been my friend longer than anyone; and my little sister, Leigh, all stood waiting on my side. Dakota's best friend, Rusty; two military buddies, Shawn and Reggi; and a close friend from his work, Leo, stood waiting for him on the opposite side. In the center stood the wedding officiate we had chosen to marry us in a black western suit, boots, and a white cowboy hat.

The final song before the service began to play. Celeste's young son, Erin, walked up to the runner wearing a tiny suit and cowboy hat. He was closely followed by Rusty's daughter, Rose, in a dress that matched my bride's maids. She threw a mix of red and white rose petals along the runner.

Next in line was Dakota in a black suit, black shirt, and red vest. He escorted his mother on one arm and my mother on the other. He kissed each on the cheek as they found their seats at the front of the crowd.

"Here Comes the Bride" began to play on the speakers a bit louder than the rest of the music. That was my queue. I exited the house carrying the bouquet that my mom had made. My dad held my left arm, and my stepdad held my right.

My dress was Western style. It was white with red flowers, making a pattern from the bust down to the skirt. My veil hung from my white cowboy hat, and my long, wavy hair was visible beneath it. I walked carefully down the aisle in my narrow-heeled white cowboy boots with two of my favorite men for support. This was it. All my dreams were coming true!

The crowd hushed, and the walk down the aisle seemed to take forever. I gazed at the man I was to marry standing under the arch, awaiting me at the end of the aisle. This was really happening! My escorts deposited me next to the love of my life, each placing a kiss on my cheek. The music stopped, and we joined hands as the officiate began the traditional ceremony.

"Dearly Beloved, we are gathered here today..."

Dakota: I couldn't believe I was actually getting married. I had been single for so long and had never dreamed that this would happen, yet here I was. Everything had moved so quickly. Here I was, watching the woman of my dreams be escorted down the aisle towards me by her dad and stepdad. I had never been so happy in my life. The ceremony went quickly and exactly as planned. It all seemed like a blur. Then there were the final words. "I now pronounce you man and wife. You may kiss the bride." The words snapped me back to reality, and I kissed the woman whom I was going to spend the rest of my life with.

Then came the barrage of hugs, well-wishes, and photos. We had the reception in the backyard, which was lined with tables. Everyone enjoyed a meal of barbecue and salads. We did the traditional thing and smashed a piece of cake in each other's face, to the pleasure of our guests. We both laughed as we smeared frosting on each other's noses. After the meal and the toasts from the Best Man and Maid of Honor, we headed to the loft for the dance. Our wedding party and families had decorated the loft, and we had yet to see it. The photographer waited for our entry, and the guests gave us time to take it in before joining us.

Solange: I had a strange, now slightly familiar, tingling sensation throughout my body as we neared the loft stairs. I brushed it off as nerves and followed my new husband up the stairs. To our delight, the rafters were strewn with dancing red and white lights, straw bales and benches lined the walls, and the center of the floor was cleared for dancing. Across the back wall, the DJ equipment was set up right next to the old player piano, which someone had cleaned up. I gasped at the sight. The tingling sensation increased. Right at that moment, the photographer snapped a shot of us. My grasp on Dakota's hand tightened, and he immediately noticed.

He gave me a puzzled look. "You, OK?"

I quickly recovered and smiled back at him brightly. "It's just so beautiful!"

Our DJ joined us as we finished surveying the scene and approached his equipment. He clicked it on, as well as another set of lights, displaying a banner with both of our first names and our now shared last name. "Ladies and Gentlemen, if you would please join us in the loft, let's get this party started!" Our guests filed up the stairs and made themselves comfortable, waiting for our first dance. The DJ played a few songs. Once everyone had filed in, the music stopped. "Ladies and Gentlemen, let's welcome the new Mr. and Mrs. Ogden to the dance floor for their first dance!"

We made our way to the center of the floor, where a spotlight shone. The first few notes of our song, the same song I had sung the night we got engaged, came through the speakers. I closed my eyes and leaned into my husband—happiness radiating through my entire body.

Suddenly, it felt like I was being electrocuted. My dress was no longer my own, and I felt shorter and smaller. The dress I wore looked like something from a long-ago past. It was no longer Dakota I was dancing with, but a younger, nicely dressed version of the farmer with the wicked eyes I was sure I had been seeing. His eyes now shone with adoration, and his features softened.

The DJ equipment was no longer there. Instead, the player piano was playing as someone sang an old tune along with it. Our guests were no longer present. The floor was filled with unfamiliar faces in old-fashioned clothing. The loft floor looked … new… and so did the rafters. *Where was I? Better yet, WHO was I?* This seemed oddly like the dream I had months earlier! I blinked my eyes hard several times. As quickly as it had happened, it was gone again! As I laid my head on Dakota's shoulder and pressed my body closer to his, I began to wonder if I was losing my sanity!

Seeing these people was beginning to become a regular occurrence! Knowing I couldn't tell anyone without it sounding like I was delusional was painful! A tear slid down my cheek as the thought lingered. I could not allow Dakota to know what was happening to me, or I might end up divorced before our marriage had even begun.

Life After Marriage

Solange: We returned from our honeymoon a week later and resumed work on the farm and normal life. A few weeks later, our wedding photos arrived in the mail. I smiled as I looked through them. That is until I came across the photo that had been snapped as we entered the loft next to the player piano. There was a strange glare in the back of the piano. It was long and tall but shapeless. I squinted and stared... The glare began to take the shape of a man... there were no features, but to me, it certainly looked to be a man! I quickly dropped the stack of photos... the photo of Dakota and I's first dance landed on top. In that photo, Dakota looked normal, but I was blurry...

Was this a coincidence, or was it proof of what had happened? Was this something I could show Dakota and maybe tell him what was happening to me? Would he accept it and try to help me figure it out, or would he think I was crazy? I quickly picked up the photos, put them in their sheath, and threw them in the drawer, deciding to look at them another time.

Six months had passed since our wedding. We were happy, typical newlyweds working to make our fixer-upper acreage into a home. I enjoyed making plans with my new husband and working on the improvements together. All the rooms in the house were now painted, and we had pulled all the linoleum from the main-level floors. We had decided to sand and refinish the hardwood floors, as after the buffing, they still bore the wear marks of many years of feet treading on them. We opted to leave the kitchen as it was until we could remodel it entirely.

I had taken on the task of cleaning up the flowerbeds, planting a garden, and trying to bring the ailing fruit trees back to life. The flowerbeds had taken some time. I removed all the old landscaping elements and re-tilled each bed. Then, I planted roses, peonies, daylilies, daisies, and several types of ground cover. With Dakota's help, I bordered each bed with railroad ties and surrounded the plants with wood chips. I even placed a new flowerbed around the base of the windmill and painted the fence around the front of the house white.

The garden was a lot of work. We broke ground in what appeared to be the foundation of an old, long-gone building. Mother Nature had reclaimed what was left and filled it with dirt over the years. There was nothing left of the building but the footings. The ground was full of grass, and the old red tiller struggled to break up the clumps of sod. We actually had to run over the plot twice with the big tiller and a third time with a smaller tiller before I was able to plant my vegetables. We lined the old foundation with landscaping bricks and used some to make rows. It now looked absolutely beautiful. With all the improvements and the new plants beginning to grow, the place was starting to look... happy!

I had a bit of a 'love-hate' relationship with the little grove of fruit trees. I loved their beauty, especially this time of the year when the leaves were growing in and the blossoms were beginning to grow. The hate part came from the same reason I avoided the hayloft of the barn. That now familiar feeling of someone watching. The physical symptoms and the mental anguish of feeling crazy that came with it. Though I had no further 'visions,' that feeling persisted. It caused chills to run up and down my spine every time. I was now able to mostly ignore it. I had to convince myself it was 'just my imagination' to keep myself sane. Every time I touched the aging trees, I felt the chill.

I forced myself to continue. These trees and the buildings were all that was left of the original farm. I had managed to get the lilac bushes trimmed, and now they looked like round, well-manicured bushes again. The flower buds had just begun to show. I had pruned all the fruit trees, other than the big pear. I had placed fertilizer spikes beside each fruit tree and began watering them daily. They were starting to show signs of recovery. I had placed landscaping timbers around each tree and wood chips inside them to hold more moisture in.

As I went to move the water to the last tree, the largest of the apples, I noticed a strange pickup entering our driveway. The driver's side window was rolled down, and an older man waved out the open window. It was a friendly face, but one I did not recognize.

The old man stopped his truck and parked it just inside the driveway. My husband wasn't home, so I was a bit concerned about this male visitor whom I had never met before. Friendly or not, he was still a stranger.

"Hello," he called in a friendly voice. He exited his pickup and walked towards me slowly. I still held the hose. I figured, worst case, I could squirt him with the hose to slow him down if need be.

"Hello, can I help you?" I responded cautiously. I didn't move as he slowly approached me.

He was dressed in an old pair of overalls, rubber boots over the legs, and a John Deere baseball cap. He was slightly stooped and walked very slowly. I could soon tell that he was not a threat. He introduced himself as Rufus Greer, the father of the previous owner. He explained that he had owned the place prior to his daughter and her now ex-husband. He had given his daughter the place after his wife had passed away from cancer. Then he moved to town.

His wife had made apple pies every year they had lived on the farm from the very tree that I was about to water. He said that they had only been on the farm for about five years before the cancer was discovered. His wife had died shortly after.

The purpose of Rufus' visit was to ask if he could get some apples from the tree after the first freeze when they became sweet. He referred to the apples as the best and sweetest he had ever eaten. He just wanted to continue the tradition that his dear wife had created. I decided that I liked the kind old man. I offered to bring him some apples, as well as bake him a pie. I thought we might become quick friends.

Rufus was ready to be on his way. He smiled a slow, easy grin and told me I reminded him of his daughter. He gave me a hug and started to amble back to his truck. He stopped halfway and lifted a bony finger, turning back to me. "One more thing before I go. I feel that I need to tell you something. People don't seem to stay in this place long. Every time someone starts to make improvements to this place, things seem to start going wrong. My wife was healthy as a horse through 35 years of marriage. Then we moved to this place to be closer to our farmland. My wife got cancer and died shortly after that."

"My daughter was newly married and happy when I gave them the place. They started to take down wallpaper, and soon after that, they started having problems. Then they got divorced after only five years."

"I like you, young lady. If things start to go haywire for you and that young man, you may want to consider moving. I can see that you two have already started to make improvements." With that, Rufus finished his short speech and continued his slow trek back to his pickup.

My jaw dropped. I had no idea what to say. He stood with his hand on the door handle of his old pickup for a moment longer as if waiting for a response. His eyes seemed to grow a bit sad, and his smile drooped.

"Thank you," I said quietly as I watched him get in his pickup and drive away. The words of the lady in my dream rang in my head. "It has only just begun." I thought about the changes in my relationship with Dakota since we moved here. Specifically, the fight that had terminated our relationship with my pastor.

I thought of the troubles that Dakota and I had begun to have. I thought of the improvements we had made, and the timing of our issues beginning. The coincidences were starting to pile up. *At what point were they no longer coincidences?* Could there *really* be something going on with this farm? The thought that a place could affect relationships and people's health seemed insane. Then again, so did the visions and the dream.

I placed the still-running hose on the tree to water it. I decided to tell Dakota that I had met the old man, but not about the warning he had given me. I also decided that I needed a dog to at least warn me when unexpected visitors were coming onto our property.

Dakota and I discussed the visit that evening. I told him about making friends with Rufus and that I planned on making him a pie when the apples were ready. We decided to look at the local Humane Society for a puppy.

A Visit from the In-laws

Solange: Dakota's family hadn't visited the place since the wedding and wanted to see the improvements we had made. His Dad, Robert, and Mom, Leona, had made plans to come stay with us in two weeks. The guest room had been painted, but the floor only had an area rug; we hadn't replaced the carpet yet.

The house was a mess from all the recent work. There were things that needed to be put away and decorations that needed to be rehung. The bed in the guest room still needed bedding. I figured that the cleanup process would probably take at least a week.

Dakota seemed nervous and agitated by the thought of his parents staying with us. This reminded me of how he had been acting prior to our first big fight, which put me on edge as well. We were both working full-time and a lot of overtime. We were both exhausted, but we knew the work had to be completed.

Dakota had been helping, but he definitely was not happy about it. He grumbled more with each task. Finally, there were only two tasks left: getting the groceries and mowing the yard. Dakota had the day before his parents arrived off from work, but I had to work a full shift. We had agreed that he would mow the lawn while I was at work, and I would grab groceries as well as some to-go burgers for supper that night. That way, everything would be done, and we could relax for the evening before our company arrived.

Work did not go as planned that day. I had a late customer, which ended up keeping me an hour after I was supposed to be done. I got out as soon as I could, grabbed the groceries and burgers, and then headed home.

It was about 7:30 pm when I got home. I noticed that the lawn had not been mowed. I parked the Cutlass and headed into the house. Dakota lay on the couch, snoring. I groaned, walked over to the couch, and shook his shoulder. He blinked as he woke. "You were supposed to mow the lawn," I said, clearly annoyed.

"Crap! I fell asleep!" He replied.

"Come on, Dakota! I worked all day, got groceries, and even brought home food! All you had to do was mow!"

I watched his face change from sleepy to angry. "Fine! I'll mow the damn lawn!" He grumbled. He was up and out the door before I could say anything else. I heard the old lawn mower fire up and start moving across the yard.

I sat down with a bottle of beer in hand. It felt like another big fight was brewing, and this one was on the evening before Dakota's parents were to arrive. I took a long swig of beer and sighed. I was afraid that this was not going to go well. I was just finishing my second beer when I heard it; clink-clink, crash! The bay window was open, so I could hear that the sound had come from near the driveway.

The lawn mower was parked next to the house and was shut off. Dakota was just getting off the seat. "Lawn's mowed," he grumbled.

"What was that sound? It sounded like something broke!" I asked, concerned.

"What sound? All I could hear was the mower," he replied.

I rolled my eyes and groaned. I walked around the house and didn't see anything damaged or broken. His car, my 69 Cutlass, and the pickup looked fine. My 84 Cutlass was parked on the far side of the driveway. The driver's side was fine, but as I neared the passenger side, I saw what I had heard from the house. There was a series of small dents running from the front fender all the way down the rear fender of my car, and my passenger-side window was shattered. The only thing holding it together was the tint. I was furious! I stormed over to Dakota. It was obvious what had happened. He had gotten too close to the side of the driveway while mowing and peppered my car with rocks. "Look what you did to my car!" I yelled.

"What?" he asked, seemingly oblivious.

"Dakota! The passenger side is all dented up, and you broke my window!"

"All I did was mow the lawn like you asked me to." He continued to insist that he had done nothing wrong. It was obvious from his tone that he was displeased at being asked to complete the task. His face couldn't hide his annoyance. He smiled, but it was more of a sneer. At that moment, he didn't look like the man that I had married at all.

"Look, Dakota, it's your parents coming to visit. I asked you to do one thing while I was at work. Now, because you threw a fit about it like a three-year-old, my show car is all dented up, and the window is broken out!"

He puffed out his chest and yelled sharply, "I didn't do anything other than mow the yard! Even if I had hurt your 'precious' car, that's all it is. A damn car!" and snickered as he walked away.

Of all the things he could have said at that time, this was the worst. Anyone who knew me knew that car was much more than just a car to me. It was what gave me the most pride of anything I had ever accomplished.

If it hadn't been for his parents arriving early the next day, I would have left again. As it was, I knew I could not. Instead, I stormed inside and locked myself in our bedroom. He could sleep on the couch. I didn't eat any of the food I had brought home. I just stayed in our room for the rest of the night. I lay there in our bed, sleepless, most of the night. I was filled with resentment for Dakota. I couldn't imagine having to face him at that moment. It felt like he had no understanding of me and a complete lack of respect after the day's events.

I woke up early the next morning, determined to appear happy for no reason other than to avoid questions from Dakota's parents. I backed my car against the tree line and closed the door carefully so as not to cause the shattered glass to separate from the tint, leaving the interior unprotected. I went to the backyard and set up the firepit and the yard furniture for the arrival of Dakota's family. He was still asleep on the couch.

My in-laws were scheduled to arrive within the hour. I had a large breakfast casserole ready to go in the oven. I quickly placed it in the oven and set the table. The plan was to have brunch in the house, then grill steaks outside for supper. I lit some incense and went to wake Dakota. I shook his shoulder. He looked up at me as if confused.

"Your folks are going to be here within the hour. You need to get showered and dressed," I said coldly.

His eyes shot open in panic. "Shoot! I overslept again!"

Before he could continue, I interrupted. "OK, here's how this is going to go. I'm very angry with you for multiple reasons. We don't have time to deal with this before your folks get here, so we aren't going to. We are going to handle this the same way we handled our fight before counseling." I stomped away to check brunch and then got myself ready for the company using the large mirror in our bedroom so that Dakota could shower.

As I looked in the mirror, I noticed the large dark bags under my eyes. I hadn't slept much the night before. I knew I had to steele myself for the visit and put on my best 'happy face' if I were going to get through the weekend without having to explain the situation to his parents. We would deal with what happened privately once they left.

I dabbed concealer under my eyes, carefully chose some eye shadow to accent my eyes and take the attention away from my puffy under eyes, and then finished the look by brushing a light coat of powder over my face. My lack of sleep was almost unnoticeable.

The doorbell rang as I walked down the stairs. I stopped for a moment, took a deep breath, and continued down the stairs. Thankfully, Dakota had already answered the door and was dressed presentably in his favorite blue polo with black stripes and jeans. His short hair was still noticeably damp.

I greeted them with a warm smile as they entered our home. I sat politely in the living room and listened to their conversation, participating occasionally.

As we moved to the dining room for brunch, I noticed Robert looking at me suspiciously. I quickly looked away. We sat around the table, each couple beside each other on opposite sides of the table. When Robert requested that we all join hands for a prayer prior to the meal, I hesitated as Dakota reached for my hand. His eyes grew cold with anger as if in warning for a brief moment. My eyes blazed back. I did reach over and link hands with him and then Robert, on the other side of the table. Again, Robert was staring at me.

We finished brunch quietly. Leona and I took a walk around the property. I left Dakota and Robert in the house to visit. I showed Leona around the property and pointed out the improvements we had made since the wedding.

As we headed towards the house, I saw Dakota and Robert standing beside my car. Dakota's head hung down, and Robert's hands rested firmly on his hips. I stopped where we were at. Leona looked at me questioningly. The men did not see us.

"You better apologize to your wife, or you're not going to have a wife much longer. No wonder she has been so quiet." Robert scolded Dakota.

Though much older and thinner than Dakota, Robert was still intimidating when he spoke. I remembered Dakota telling me in a previous conversation that Robert had been a Drill Sergeant in the Army when he was a young man. I imagined that carried through when he needed to reprimand his son. Dakota clearly knew that he was wrong by the look on his face and his defeated posture.

The words of my father-in-law in his thick southern accent warmed my heart. Tears welled up in my eyes. I left Leona standing where she was and took off at a run for the tree grove. I really didn't know why I felt the need to go that way, but that's where instinct pointed me.

I found myself sitting under the pear tree with my head buried in my lap, crying. I felt a hand on my shoulder. I thought maybe it was Dakota or one of his parents coming to check on me. As I looked up, what I saw was not a living person but the same woman whom I had now seen several times. She wasn't solid, yet not completely transparent.

Tears ran down her face. She held up her arms, and I could see bruises on them, as if she had been tied up. One eye appeared bruised. She opened her mouth as if to say something. As she did, I could hear footsteps approaching. Then, *he* appeared out of nowhere and grabbed her by one of her bruised wrists. *He* began to pull her away.

It was the same old farmer I had also seen several times before. His face appeared twisted with anger. Before he could pull her away, she pointed one finger towards the tree grove on the other side of the driveway where my car was parked. Then, they were both gone as quickly as they appeared.

I didn't know if I felt scared or surprised. Again, I wondered if the stress was causing me to lose my mind. Now, Dakota stood in front of me. He looked very sorry. He did, in fact, apologize very sincerely for what he had done to my car.

I now had another reason to be shaken. I told my family that I just needed some time and would be back soon. Luckily, they understood. Before I left, I grabbed the sheath containing our wedding photos out of the drawer I had deposited them. I hopped in my 69 Cutlass and headed to Celeste's house. The old lady and the wicked-looking old man I presumed to be her husband had appeared too many times. It had to be Cecil and Matilda! I had to tell someone.

Luckily, Celeste's son and his dad were out at the arcade for the evening so that we could talk alone. I had called her before I left, explaining the fight, the in-laws, and that there was something else that I didn't want to discuss over the phone.

I hadn't told anyone about any of the 'sightings,' as I had begun to call them, or the dream. She had a 'sixth sense' with things such as this, so I knew she would be safe to tell and maybe even help me figure out what was going on.

Celeste greeted me at the door with a beer. We both plopped down in lawn chairs near the fire she had already started. She didn't seem surprised as I recounted each time I had seen the farmer and his wife. Not even when I pulled out the pictures from our wedding with the strange anomalies. Celeste sat quietly, sipping her beer and occasionally nodding as I told her that, at several points, it had felt as if I had been someone else.

Finally, she spoke. "I have felt a strange presence every time I have gotten near that barn since the first time I visited you there. I've also felt the change in you and Dakota. The first thing we need to do is get rid of that piano."

We decided to use the excuse of needing the hay-loft to store hay for the horses, as well as making more room for parties up there. We would push the piano out of the big hay loft door and haul the pieces to the fire pit to be burnt. For the moment, the plan would have to wait. I needed to return home and deal with the questions my in-laws were sure to have and figure out what to do about the damage to my car, as well as to our relationship. My best friend hugged me and sent me on my way. I felt much better after finally revealing my secret. We also had a plan as to how to deal with the problem.

I returned home with renewed confidence. I still felt a bit uncertain about the fight between Dakota and me. It felt like the tension between him and I was increasing. At least I knew that Robert and Celeste understood. When I got home, the family was sitting around the fire. Thankfully, Leona had helped Dakota put together supper, and they had saved me a plate. I didn't attempt to put on a fake smile this time. I just walked up to the group and sat down. I explained to our family that we both had been under a lot of pressure and apologized for it escalating in front of them. Dakota did seem genuinely sorry. We agreed just to enjoy the rest of our weekend.

The tensions eased, and the conversation began to flow easily. I found myself smiling as I described the work we had accomplished as a team. Eventually, I allowed my hand to relax on Dakota's leg. I caught Robert's expression as his straight face turned into a knowing grin.

Our company left on Monday. I hugged Leona tightly. I had actually enjoyed her company after everything had settled down. She moved to her son, and Robert came to my side. "Thank you so much," I whispered in his ear. Although Leona was growing on me, I really loved the old southern gentleman, who I was lucky enough to call my father-in-law!

As we embraced, he placed something in my hand. "This should be enough to cover what that bonehead son of mine did to your car." I didn't look at what was in my hand; I just placed it in my pocket. "Don't let this get between the two of you. I think you two have a good thing going, but if he ever does something like this again, don't be afraid to call." His blue eyes looked a bit misty behind his glasses as we said goodbye one more time before they crawled into their car. Robert rolled down his window, waved, and honked his horn as they left.

I reached into my pocket. There were ten one-hundred-dollar bills. More than enough to fix my car. "Your Dad just saved us a ton of money." I pulled the money from my pocket and showed it to Dakota.

"I really am sorry if that means anything." His eyes and body language said that he meant it.

"I forgive you, but if you ever hurt my car again, forgiveness may not come so easy," I said with a glint of remaining anger in my eyes.

Now that I knew my car was going to be ok, I was excited about the idea of getting rid of the piano and, hopefully, the unwanted visits from the farmer and his wife. I pitched the idea of a summer party with all our friends and burning the piano as part of the festivities.

Dakota seemed excited for the party but reluctant to destroy the piano. He claimed that he wanted to save it and restore it someday. His face seemed to change when talking about it. I just wanted it gone. I decided to stop talking about it and do it when the party rolled around.

The night of the party, the front yard quickly filled up with our friends' vehicles. Aside from our wedding, this had to be the biggest party on the farm to date. The recently purchased above-ground pool was full. In it was a floating cooler full of various types of alcohol and soda. There were also several inflatable pool toys to lounge on and a floating light that spun merrily near the water circulating from the pump.

The big yard light illuminated the yard. The dug-out firepit was piled high with discarded wood we had gathered while cleaning the place up. In the center was an old, discarded couch. A set of large house speakers bordered the fire pit, and bass from the music pumped through them, rattling the house windows. I had set up several long tables nearby with chips, dip, salads, and desserts. As people filled the yard, they each brought additional dishes to add.

I was busy cooking burgers, brats, and ribs on the grill for the main course. It was a party that would have earned us a visit from the police, had it not been in the middle of nowhere! The mood was jovial!

People started to find seats around the firepit. Dakota squirted most of a bottle of lighter fluid onto the discarded couch. He struck a wooden match and threw it at the pit. The sofa went up in a ball of flames, making a loud woof sound. The crowd of friends cheered as a few who were too close to the firepit jumped back. Now, the party had officially begun.

As the night progressed, people sat drinking, eating, and visiting. A few splashed in the pool. I made rounds to each group, eventually finding Celeste and the perfect opportunity to sneak away from the party.

We quietly snuck away from the busy group towards the barn. We knew the hated piano would be heavy, but we figured we could roll it out of the small door in the loft. I hoped with the music and the conversation that, the noise of the piano hitting the ground would go unnoticed. I also hoped that the piano would break into enough pieces that it would be easy to throw in the fire without being noticed.

We both knew the plan, so there wasn't any conversation. We wanted to get it done quickly. I was anxious to see if ridding the farm of the piano would rid me of my ghost farmer problem. Since my first experience with my unwanted friends had taken place in the loft with the piano, I thought that destroying the piano was a good place to start.

I held my finger to my lips to quiet Celeste. She had begun to giggle when I tripped over a rock heading to the barn. We were both tipsy at this point, but we had a task to accomplish. We finally made it to the barn and up the stairs to the loft. We hadn't been spotted.

There it sat. Just as it had since we moved in and probably for many years before. The creepy feeling I had experienced so many times before was no longer there. It was replaced with something else: relief. *Was it because of the alcohol? Was it because I had my best friend with me? Was it just hope that the farm could finally feel normal? Or were the feelings even my own?*

I carefully opened the smaller loft door. It creaked, but the barn was far enough from the party that there was no way anyone could have heard it. "OK, let's do this," I said to my best friend, finally breaking the silence.

We first had to turn the piano sideways so that it could fit out the door. The thing was heavy. We grunted at its weight. We managed to get it to the edge of the door. The piano teetered on the edge of the door, almost as if fighting for its very existence. Celeste took action and gave it the final shove. It slid the rest of the way out of the loft door and quickly plunged to the ground. It hit the ground, and a barrage of off-key notes sounded, as well as the shattering of wood. Celeste and I shot each other mischievous smiles.

"Do you feel any different?" she asked me.

I stopped, took a deep breath, and closed my eyes. "No… Not really," I said, almost disappointed.

"Well, maybe that's a good thing. You don't see them anywhere, do you?" she asked.

I looked around and shrugged. "Nope, just you and me in a hay loft." We hoped for the best. Neither of us felt anything, so all we could do was hope that I wouldn't see any more of the ghost couple.

Then, the realization hit that we needed to dispose of the evidence. We made our way out of the loft to the front of the barn, where the piano lay shattered into pieces. We gathered as many pieces as possible and hurried back to the now large bonfire in the yard. By this point in the evening, most of the partygoers had consumed plenty of beverages, and what was being thrown into the fire was no longer important. Just that the fire stayed going. Luckily, this included Dakota. He had failed to notice the destruction of the piano. Over the rest of the evening, the piano disappeared.

That night, I slept peacefully. Dakota, however, was very restless. I could feel him tossing and turning. I woke up before him, which was very unusual.

Friends were picking up tents and crawling out of campers. I felt rested for the first time in a long time.

I decided to make a large breakfast for everyone. I whipped up a pot of coffee, put it into a thermos, and then made a second one. I also made two bake pans full of breakfast burritos and some hash browns patties with cheese.

As I was finishing up, my closest male friend, Lawrence, stumbled into the kitchen. He had been sleeping on the couch in the four-season porch. The smell of breakfast had woken him. His long black hair hung in loose curls below his shoulders instead of being contained in its usual ponytail. He brushed a strand off one of his high cheekbones. His milk chocolate brown eyes looked bloodshot as he removed his glasses and rubbed them with a yawn.

"Mornin, I didn't realize you stayed," I said with a smile.

"Ya. I wasn't going to drive anywhere after that much to drink. I didn't figure you would mind if I crashed in here," he said. We shared a warm smile.

At that moment, Celeste stumbled through the kitchen door, looking very unhappy. "Roman left me sleeping in your camper, and now I don't have a way home. I have no idea when or why he left," she whined.

I rolled my eyes. "You really know how to pick 'em. Don't worry. I'll give you a ride home. Let's get some food to everyone and make sure they all get out of here. Then I'll take you home."

The remainder of the party people had eaten and slowly disbursed. That left Celeste, Lawrence, and I in the kitchen. Dakota was still not up. We decided to wander around the property for a bit and wait to see if he got up before I left to take Celeste home. Surprisingly, there wasn't much of a mess left after the party. The fire was burnt down to ashes but still smoldering. Luckily, no sign of the piano remained.

As we neared the tree grove, I started to feel nauseous, and breathing became more difficult. "Guys, I think last night is catching up to me," I said and stopped for a moment. I bent over and placed my hands on my knees. I began to feel a bit better. Celeste and Lawrence had let me stand still for a bit and continued walking around on their own. I composed myself and started towards the spot in the trees where my friends were now standing, looking up at something.

The morning sunshine glinted off something in the direction they were looking. Then the headache set in. I found the sudden onset of my symptoms very odd since I had felt so rested and good at the start of the day. I tried to ignore the splitting pain and shielded my eyes from the sun with my hands as I approached my friends. "What are you guys looking at?" I questioned.

"There is some sort of lock grown into this tree," Lawrence said with surprise.

I saw it, too, when they pointed to it. It was pretty large and mostly rusted. As I stood directly under the branch with the lock grown into it, a stabbing pain behind my eyes caused me to wince and double over again. "I'm sorry, guys, I'm not feeling well at all. I guess I'm more hungover than I thought," I said. I asked Lawrence if he could give Celeste a ride home so that I didn't have to drive, and I went inside to lie down as soon as they left.

It was late in the afternoon when I woke up. To my surprise, Dakota stood over me, and he looked angry. His presence may have woken me. It took me a moment to realize he was holding something. "What's up?" I asked sleepily.

He held what looked like a metal tube with a solid rod connected to each side. In the other hand, was something that looked white, but charred. "What did you do to my piano?" he growled through gritted teeth.

"Your... piano?" I asked. I was confused. When my eyes focused, I realized that he was holding a charred piano key in one hand and what must have been the scroll from the player piano that Celeste and I had destroyed the night before.

"What... How.... Why do you even care? I didn't think it was any big deal... It made more room in the loft. Besides, the thing was creepy." I sputtered as I spoke. I moved from laying on the couch to sitting and backed away from him. I could feel his anger. For the first time, I was scared of him. He was a huge man, and I knew he could hurt me if he wanted. "Since when is it your piano?" I finally finished.

He threw down the pieces of the piano and raised his hands as if he were going to strangle me. "That piano was a wedding gift to us! How can it mean so little to you?" His voice seemed to change, and his speech pattern didn't seem to be normal.

I pulled my knees to my chest and raised my hands in front of my face. I got as small as I could into the corner of the couch to try to protect myself in case he actually intended to hurt me. "What are you talking about?" I said quietly. Now, I was really scared. This wasn't at all like Dakota. He had never raised his hands to me before. "That piano was here when we moved in. We saw it for the first time when we looked at this place!" I said. It seemed like he hadn't heard me.

"You destroyed our wedding gift!" He stepped closer. I quickly ducked as his hands went for my neck. Our puppy, Stryker, charged at him, barking and growling. Dakota kicked the puppy, and he let out a yelp.

"Dakota, what are you doing?!" I yelled in alarm. I scooped up my puppy and backed towards the door. As I did, he shook his head as if trying to wake up. Then, his face changed. His hands dropped, and he looked down at them as if he had never seen his own hands before.

"What... am I doing down here, and why do you look so scared?" Dakota asked.

My surprise could not be hidden. "You were just screaming at me about the piano."

"What? What about the piano? I just woke up!" He looked sleepy and confused.

"Dakota... you're really scaring me. What is going on? You seriously don't remember trying to strangle me and kicking Stryker? You said I destroyed our wedding present?"

"Seriously? I just woke up! I have no idea how I got down here! The last thing I remember is that I was in our bed. I was having this really weird dream, but I can't remember anything about it!"

Then it hit me... *Destroying the piano hadn't helped; it had made the ghosts angry! How could I make this better?* Though she had only left hours before, I missed Celeste. This problem was going to require more of her 'special talent' to figure out. My fear changed to concern for Dakota when I realized how confused he was.

"OK, it's OK. You must have been sleepwalking," I said. Stryker looked up at me and wined. I put him down, and he skittered away.

"I'm so sorry!" Dakota said. He stood beside me, looking at his hands again. "I would never try to hurt you."

"I know. I think I'm going to go stay at Celeste's. I know you didn't mean anything, but I need some time. You're a lot bigger than me, and you could have really hurt me." I walked away as I spoke. I got to our room and called Celeste.

"Hello," she answered, sounding tired.

"This is not good!" I started and proceeded to rattle off what had happened. "I think destroying the piano made it worse!" He tried to strangle me and didn't remember doing it."

Celeste: I had only left Solange's house a few hours ago. I had my own problems to deal with. Roman was being a dick again and hadn't even apologized for leaving me sleeping in the camper. I knew that Solange needed me. Sometimes having a sixth sense was a pain in the ass.

"OK, come on over," I said through the phone. I rolled my eyes. Roman was still ignoring me, and I wasn't going to be the one to break the silence. It wasn't me who had left the party without a word. I would deal with him when he decided to quit pouting about whatever he was sulking about.

Our son was in his room playing video games, and I hoped he could entertain himself. I also secretly hoped that Solange didn't want to stay the night. I was exhausted from the party. I also really had no idea how to help. There had to be something else on the property, causing my best friend to suffer. I had to help her find it.

Matilda: I watched the young woman leave. I had been trying so hard to warn her. Warn her about my fate, my husband, and this place... I did not want to see yet another young couple suffer the same fate I had seen happen so many times before.

I didn't know that I had died until I was somehow looking down at my own lifeless, bloodied body. My husband stood over me, his chest heaving with each breath. The last thing I remembered was feeling helpless. He had me chained to a tree with a lock securing me there. My arms had quit hurting several hours ago, as blood flowing to them had stopped with them chained above my head. My legs felt heavy, and my feet ached. My knees threatened to buckle, but only slightly bent. I was not able to pull myself up, nor kneel, or sit. I was stuck standing there, chained to a branch of a tree, hidden amongst the thick grove. My husband, the one person who was supposed to love me above all others, stood in front of me, screaming about how losing everything was my fault.

This had been going on for months and getting progressively worse. At first, he just beat me while chained and let me go with the threat that he would kill me if I tried to escape or tell anyone. I hid the bruises with clothing or my hair as well as I could. I never went to town, and my friends had stopped coming by due to his cruelty to them and me. My parents had both passed away one right after the other a year or so ago. Now, I had no one other than Cecil. My life had become a nightmare.

Cecil handled business with the one hired man we had left and went to town for any supplies we needed. To the outside world, nothing had changed any more than it had for any other struggling farmer.

The abuse got worse. He started locking me in the cellar when I was not chained to the tree. My once large, strong frame was shrinking. I was no longer making the meals. He was making what he knew how to make out of the meager supplies we had left stored and what little we could afford to buy. I was only allowed to eat his scraps. My body was shrinking. I was slowly starving… wasting away.

Then it happened. He stopped yelling. He looked at me with a blank look in his eyes. Cecil reached behind his back and produced a small revolver. I watched in horror as the scene unwound as if in slow motion. He leveled the gun at my head and cocked the hammer. I screamed, but it did no good. I heard the click as he pulled the trigger, and my world went dark.

As the world around me came back into focus. Everything seemed brighter. I no longer felt the heaviness of my arms or the pain in my legs and feet. I blinked a couple of times and realized I was no longer chained to the tree. I was... floating. I looked down, and there I was... or my body, anyway. My body was still chained to the tree. Cecil stood in front of my body, still holding the gun. In his other hand was a piece of paper. I saw him place the paper in the front pocket of his overalls, where it was still partially visible. Then he placed the muzzle of the revolver into his own mouth and pulled the trigger.

Then, he was there with me, looking at both of our bodies. My nightmare continued, to my horror. We have both been here on this property since that day. I felt trapped. I had tried to leave. Each time I try, I end up floating by that tree where I died. The lock is still there. The chain now rusted... My body and Cecil's body...long gone.

Cecil leaves me mostly alone unless I try to speak to him or interfere with his torment of each new inhabitant of our home. After discovering he could still affect the living world even in death, he became equally as much of a terror in death as he had been in life. The longer we remained, the stronger he became and the more tricks he discovered. I tried to help, but I was simply not as strong as he was.

This time, as the farm's newest inhabitants started to turn on each other, I tried harder. I was determined to save these people and maybe even release myself from this never-ending cycle of hell in the process.

Solange: The stereo in my 69 Cutlass couldn't go loud enough to drown the thoughts in my head as I tore down the blacktop towards Celeste's house. Stryker rested his head on my lap and looked up at me with concerned chocolate-brown eyes. I absent-mindedly patted his head. I knew Dakota truly felt that he hadn't tried to hurt me. *So, exactly what had happened?* I replayed the scene in my head again, trying to remember the events exactly as they had happened. Then I remembered sitting under the pear tree and seeing the ghostly woman pointing across the road to the large tree grove.

More questions arose in my head. *Who were the woman and the wicked-looking man that I kept seeing? Could they actually be the original owners of the farm? If so, how and why did I keep seeing them? Why had she pointed to the tree line? Was there something else there that she wanted me to see?* I thought about the headache and then spotting the lock and chain with Lawrence and Celeste. *Was that what she wanted me to see? What was the deal with the piano? Why was Dakota so mad about it that he had tried to strangle me? Our wedding present?*

I found myself almost missing my turn to Celeste's house. She was sitting on the deck in front of her trailer house, beer in hand, waiting for me. As I pulled up and opened the driver's side door, Stryker barreled out and ran up to Celeste, jumping on her lap. I opened the back door, taking my cat, Whammo, out of the car in her carrier and carrying her up to the deck with me.

Celeste sighed. "You know that Roman is allergic to cats. You can't have her in the house." She said as she pointed to the cat carrier. I had completely forgotten.

"Oops," I said, groaning. "I guess we can't stay." I was upset with myself for forgetting, but also glad I had gotten out of the house and taken the animals with me.

"So, tell me again what happened, starting from when I left. Don't leave out any details." Celeste stated as we started to talk.

I sat the cat carrier down on the deck in front of me and grabbed a cold beer from my best friend. I took a long swig before relaying the story in detail. Celeste sat quietly. I watched her expressions carefully as I explained. Finally, I finished. I took a deep breath, concerned by the look on her face.

"Well, obviously, destroying the piano wasn't the answer, so your friends weren't connected to it. There must be something else on that farm. You started feeling sick after we walked towards the trees, and it got worse when we were by the tree with the lock. That has to be part of the equation here." Celeste's forehead wrinkled with concern as she spoke. My face mirrored her own concern. "I agree with you that Dakota is being affected somehow. It seems like destroying the piano made it worse, so it must have been related. I want you guys to try something. Go stay in a motel tonight. Tell Dakota it's a date night. Kind of a way to relieve stress," she suggested.

My eyes lit up at that idea. "That's a great idea! Then we can see how he acts away from the farm." I replied while rubbing my chin in thought. I picked up my phone and called Dakota to present the idea. He still had no idea what we suspected was going on. I wanted to try getting him away from the farm to test the theory. If it held true, then I could figure out a way to tell him. I feared that we would end up having to leave our dream home. I was excited that, yet again, Celeste had come up with a possible solution. Still, a knot built in my stomach at the thought of the farm itself being the problem and having to leave after all of the work we had put into it.

Dakota agreed that a date night would be nice for just the two of us. We both put in for a vacation day from work, and Celeste agreed to look after the animals for us. I thanked her profusely and gave her a hug. It had been a short but productive visit. "I don't know what I would do without you," I told Celeste.

She smiled back at me. "I just hope we can find a solution for you guys."

I loaded the cat and dog back into the car and headed home to pick up Dakota. He said he would throw some things in a bag and be ready when I got there.

The Test

Solange: The night at the motel and our date was very pleasant. We both rested well that night. That was all the proof that I needed that the farm itself was having some effect on us. I decided to tell Dakota my thoughts while he was still in a good mood and while we were still away from the farm.

The following morning, we went to our favorite restaurant in town for breakfast. I ordered an omelet with ham, onions, and cheese with a side of hashbrowns, grilled onions, and cheese. Dakota had biscuits and gravy.

We sat in silence. Dakota must have read my mind or my body language. "What's the matter, dear? I thought we were good again after last night," he said.

I stopped chewing mid-bite and looked up at him. I could see the concern in his eyes. I swallowed hard and dropped my fork. "There is something I wanted to talk to you about.... I think we need to sell the farm." I started slowly and carefully.

"What, we both love it there; why?" he asked.

"I feel like something there is affecting both of us and not in a good way. Haven't you noticed how much more we have been fighting?" I asked.

Dakota's voice raised. I could feel the hurt and disappointment change to anger. His expression changed.

"Dakota, please... Just hear me out," I said. I reached across the table and placed my hand on his, hoping to calm him. His face was getting red now. I thought to myself that maybe doing this in public was not a good idea. "OK, let's just go home."

We finished the rest of our meal in silence. *Maybe the farm's effect had gotten to him. Could it be possible that the farm could affect us even when we weren't there?* Things did not get any better when we got home. Celeste's car was there when we pulled in.

Proof of the Curse

Cecil: I watched them pull back into the yard. To my pleasure, they did not look happy. They would be less pleased when they saw what had happened while they were away. I snickered to myself. This would definitely cause a fight. Like all the others, this couple would not get a happily ever after.

I knew I was dead. I had been for many years. What I didn't know was why I was still here. After I had pulled the trigger, everything had gone black, but then suddenly, there was light again. I was looking at my wife and myself. I was no longer in my body. I was looking at it.

Since then, I have figured out that I could not leave this place, no matter how hard I tried. What I could do, however, was affect others—affect those who were still living. I hadn't wanted others to have this farm when money issues had forced me to start selling it off piece by piece. I had wanted to destroy it. I certainly did not want anyone living their lives happily there now, after I had died, because I could not. Yes, I could affect them, and I enjoyed doing so.

Somehow, my wife, who I had killed with my own two hands, was also still here. She had no more control over me now than she had when we were alive. She could not affect the living nor stop me from doing so. It was working yet again.

Dakota: I was still pissed off as we drove home. I mean, after all, we had been through looking for a place. After finally finding the place of our dreams. After all the work we had put into trying to bring this place back to life. After... getting married here. How could she want to sell it? I was not going to go through all of that again. Over my dead body, we were selling this place.

I looked over at Solange. She sat quietly in the passenger seat of my car, hands folded in her lap, staring out the window. I felt bad for snapping at her, but not bad enough to apologize. I frowned and looked back at the road ahead. I gripped the steering wheel harder and sighed.

I noticed Celeste's car was parked near the barn as we pulled in. I knew she was going to take care of the animals while we were gone, but there was really no reason she should still be here this time of the day. "Why is Celeste still here?" I asked Solange.

She looked concerned. "I have no idea. I haven't heard anything from her since I asked her to take care of the animals. I hope she's OK." I parked the car near Celeste's and headed into the barn. "Celeste?" Solange called out.

In here," came the muffled response from the tack room. "I think your water pump sprung a leak. I can't see where it's coming from. I think it's below ground. I shut it off, but the ground keeps getting muddier! It's closer to a puddle now! I've been here for hours trying to figure out how to fix this!" Celeste sounded disgusted.

"You should have called us, Celeste," Solange said.

"I didn't want to stress you guys out while you were on your night out," she replied.

We sent Celeste on her way, and I started digging. I dug down about three feet around the water pump. I could only dig a circle close to the pump shaft as there was only a small patch of open dirt, and the rest of the floor was a cement patch. The further down we went, the more standing water we encountered. A leak was still not visible. There were no cracks on the pump shaft, and no water appeared to be leaking anywhere.

"I think we're in over our heads. We need to call Waylon." Solange said, referring to her stepdad. "He used to be a plumber, and maybe he still has his tools."

I was cold, I was wet, and I was still mad about the way our date ended, and now this. I threw down the shovel. Frustration got the best of me. "Fine, as usual, you need to call your parents instead of letting your perfectly capable husband fix the problem!" I stormed off towards the house, leaving my wife standing in the tack room with her mouth hanging wide open.

Solange: I stood in the tack room for a few minutes, feeling defeated. The trouble just never seemed to stop with this place lately. We had to re-solve the problem and sell this place, or we would end up getting a divorce. I walked over to the barn's water main to shut it off. The horses had enough water in their trough, and shutting off the water would keep more water from leaking, creating a bigger mess.

I knew Dakota did not want help, and getting help would only make him angrier; help was needed! I pulled my phone out of my pocket and dialed my mom's number. I quickly explained the situation, as well as the events of the last couple of days. We de-cided that Mom and Waylon would come over the next day, as well as enlist the help of my dad.

I didn't say anything to Dakota. I simply showered, warmed up some leftovers for myself, and went to watch TV in our room for the evening. Yet again, as what had happened with our fights in the past, Dakota never came to bed.

The next day, he still wasn't speaking to me. I just ignored him and went about my morning as usual. We both had to work. My parents had agreed to be at the farm to try to help get the hydrant fixed by the time we got home.

The workday went by uneventfully. I beat Dakota home. As promised, my mom, stepdad, and dad were waiting. Waylon's truck was backed up to the barn with tools in the bed. Waylon was a bit shorter and a bit broader than my dad. Dad was tall and wiry. They both leaned against the barn, waiting for me. Mom and Karen waited in the pickup.

"OK, let's get this done," Waylon said in his deep, gruff tone. We all entered the small tack room, and it was quickly decided that it was too small for all of us. The men decided to break up the cement in the tack room close to the hydrant so that they could dig the hole wider and deeper. They sent my mom, stepmom, and me up to the house to make supper.

I watched my dad and stepdad grab sledgehammers from the back of the pickup, and my mom, my stepmom, and I headed up to the house hesitantly. I wondered how things would go when Dakota got home. At least my parents were there if he was going to be a jerk. I wasn't one to hide behind someone else, but with the way Dakota had been acting, I was really glad my parents were there. As big as Dakota was, I knew he wouldn't dare to get out of hand with my dad and stepdad there.

Mom, Karen, and I wasted some time cleaning the kitchen up a bit and throwing together a vegetable beef stew with garlic bread. For some reason, Dakota was not home yet. "Why don't we bring some hot chocolate down to your dad and Waylon? I bet they are cold working in that mud," Mom suggested. She was always thinking of everyone else. That was one of my favorite things about her. We made up a large pot of sweet brown liquid, added mini marshmallows, filled a mug for each man, and headed to the barn.

The men had made a lot of progress! Each was now standing on one side of a hole that was a quarter as wide as the small tack room and almost as deep as Waylon was tall. Both men were covered in mud. It was even in Waylon's graying hair and on the baseball cap that covered the top of my dad's bald head. As we approached, the pile of concrete chunks chiseled out of the floor and two large piles of muddy tan clay-like dirt looked huge. I could only imagine how heavy each shovel must have been to dig out of the wet hole. I smiled, handing each man a mug. "How are you coming?" I asked. "That's a lot of dirt and concrete."

"Well, we haven't been able to find the leak yet, but we've got to be getting close. We're almost six feet down." Waylon said in his deep, gruff voice. Dad looked miserable and didn't say anything. Both men took long swigs out of their mugs.

"Thank you, both," I said, grabbing both men in a group hug. My dad finally smiled.

"Thanks, Solange. I was getting pretty cold," Dad said.

"Drink your coco, Waylon. You're going to catch a cold." My mom scolded him as she placed a coat over Waylon's muddy shirt. Waylon rolled his eyes and groaned, knowing he didn't dare object. Karen also provided my dad with a coat.

"Thank you both so much, really. I don't want to think about how much this would have cost if we would have had to pay someone," I said. My eyes welled with tears.

Both men quickly finished their warm drinks and handed me back their mugs. Waylon handed the now filthy coat back to my mom. "Time to get back to work. If we keep at it just a little longer, we should be able to get this done yet tonight. Ready, Leonard?"

Dad looked exhausted as he handed his coat back to Karen and kissed her on her cheek. Again, he did not speak but joined Waylon back in the hole.

"Supper should be ready in an hour or so. We have homemade stew in the crockpot and garlic bread." Mom said as she smiled down at the men. "Stay as warm and dry as you can and come in as soon as possible so you can get clean and warm."

Waylon stabbed his shovel into the wet, muddy ground with determination. The blade made a squishing sound as it entered the ground, and then I heard a chink sound as if it hit something other than dirt.

"What was that?" I watched as the newest shovel full of dirt landed on the pile. There was something solid in the mud. I bent over to inspect the solid clump.

As I did, a car door slammed. Dakota stumbled into the barn.

"What are they doing here? I told you I could handle this," Dakota slurred.

"Dakota, have you been drinking?" I asked.

"So what? I went out for a couple of drinks with my buddies after work. I'm fine," he replied.

I could smell the alcohol on his breath even though he was some distance away from me in the small room. "Dakota, Waylon, and my dad have experience with stuff like this. We don't. They're here to help. This could have cost us a fortune if they hadn't helped! Be nice!" I said, almost pleading. I was embarrassed by his drunken state and his attitude. My mom looked like she wanted to say something, and both Waylon and my dad looked angry.

"Well, at least let me help." Dakota stumbled and fell forward, landing with his face in the hole between Dad and Waylon.

"All right! I've seen enough! Leonard, Karen, Charlotte, help Solange get her 'husband' into the house," Waylon growled in disgust.

Dad also looked disgusted as he laid his shovel at the side of the hole and climbed out. "You should be ashamed of yourself, young man. If I were still a police officer, you would be on your way to jail right now." My dad said as he grabbed one of Dakota's arms. My mom grabbed the other.

"I can take care of myself!" Dakota began to slur.

"I think I would quit while you're ahead," my mom snapped angrily at him. All I could do was watch in embarrassment as my parents hauled my husband up off the ground and started to help him to the house. I hung my head and began to follow.

"You know, Solange, if you need help, all you have to do is ask," Waylon stated in a softer-than-normal tone. His back was turned, and he was still digging, determined to fix the problem for me.

"Thank you," was all I could muster. The meaning of his words did not go unnoticed. The problem was getting worse. Others were noticing now. Mom and Dad took Dakota to the house and up to our bedroom. Karen checked dinner while the others dealt with Dakota. Waylon finished up the project in the barn shortly afterward.

He had been right. He and Dad had not been far away from where the leak was when Mom, Karen, and I had brought the hot cocoa down to the barn. Once he had found the leak, patching the hydrant had not been difficult. It had only taken him a few more minutes. Then he came up to the house, muddy, wet, and cold, for a warm shower and some hot stew.

Dinner was awkward with my mom, dad, Waylon, and Karen. I felt like all eyes were on me. Dakota had not come down from upstairs. Waylon finally broke the silence. "We will need to turn the pump on after a bit to make sure it doesn't leak. You guys are going to need to fill in the hole," he said matter-of-factly.

I stirred my stew nervously. I had no appetite. Dakota had made a total fool of me in front of my parents. *What was going on with him? He should have known better! He worked at the jail, and if he had gotten caught, not only would he be losing his job, but he would be spending time in the same jail!* "Thank you, all of you, for your help today. I'm so sorry about Dakota's behavior." I looked around the table at each of my parents. All I could do was hope that my sincerity showed.

"I think he has a problem," my dad said quietly. "He's not thinking about you or his job. He's not thinking at all. He's just acting irresponsibly." Mom looked like she wanted to say something but was holding back.

I didn't know what to say or do. I thought quickly and decided it was best to defend my husband. "It was a one-time thing. He's been under a lot of pressure." I knew that my family could tell I was lying. What else could I do? I was caught between a rock and a hard spot.

Dinner finished quietly. Mom and Karen helped me clear the table and put the dishes away. Mom and I came face to face as we put away the last of the mess.

"If this happens again, you need to leave. He's going to kill himself or someone else driving that drunk," Mom said.

I didn't need to reply. I knew her statement came from a place of love. I knew she was right. I hugged each parent and thanked them again as they headed out. I was exhausted. I didn't even bother to shower and headed directly to bed. Dakota lay face down on the bed, snoring. To my dismay, the way he was spread out did not allow me to get in bed without disturbing him. I decided against it and headed to the spare bedroom with a heavy sigh. Despite my troubled mind, I fell asleep quickly.

Dakota was up early and out of the house before me the next morning. He returned late in the evening, finding excuses to avoid me the rest of the week. He refused to answer his phone calls or texts. I was becoming increasingly more concerned. I hoped he was not drinking more.

Celeste also seemed to be avoiding me. I hadn't been able to get her to answer her phone. The only text I had received had just stated that she was sick and would get ahold of me when she felt up to it. I kept myself busy with work and trying to keep up with everything that needed to be done around the farm.

Things had been going downhill quickly, to say the least. Gone were the days of working together on projects around the farm. Gone were the big parties with all our friends. Gone was that love bubble we had enjoyed so much. I knew we needed to talk. A deep depression was taking over me.

It turned out we were not going to get that chance to talk. One night, when it was well past time for Dakota to be home, I got a call from an unknown number. "Hello?" I answered.

"Solange, it's me." Dakota's slurred voice came from the other line.

"Dakota?"

"Ya, it's me. I need you to come get me."

"What? Why? Aren't you on your way home from work?" I was very confused.

"Just come get me at the jail." Then the line went dead.

What the hell? I thought. I dialed Dakota's cell, but it went straight to voicemail. I grabbed my keys off the hanger on the wall in the kitchen and headed for my pickup with more questions than answers in my mind.

I drove the thirteen miles to town and a few blocks to Dakota's work. The first thing that I noticed was that Dakota's car was not in the employee parking lot. I parked in the visitor parking area, walked up to the cold steel door, and hit the button for the intercom. A familiar voice came through the speaker.

"Sheriff's Office, how can I help you?"

"Joyce, it's Solange Ogden, Dakota's wife. He asked me to pick him up." I said to the receptionist through the intercom.

"I'll buzz you in. Just a moment." Came the friendly reply.

Buzz, click, the door unlocked, and I let myself in. I walked up to the front desk. "Hey, Joyce, where's Dakota?" I asked. "I didn't see him in the office area anywhere."

Her smile faded. "Well, dear, I'm afraid he wasn't calling for a ride home from work. He got picked up driving under the influence."

"What?" I replied in surprise.

"He used his phone call to reach you," Joyce replied sadly.

"That would explain the unknown number and why his cell went to voicemail when I tried to call him back." I was seeing red.

"You can speak with him, but he won't be able to leave until someone pays his bail." Joyce looked like she felt guilty about what she had just told me.

"What is bail?" I asked.

"It looks like it would be one thousand dollars," she replied.

"I'm going to kill him! I will pay for it, but he may be better off staying here!" I said angrily.

The old receptionist smiled and returned to the rear of the building, where the jail cells were located. Soon after, she returned to the front with a very ashamed-looking Dakota. His shirt was half untucked, and it was a plain button-up shirt, not the uniform shirt that he wore. I could smell the alcohol from across the counter.

He wouldn't even look at me. I handed Joyce the check for bail, and we exited the building. It was a long, silent drive home. While at the jail, I texted my boss and explained that an emergency had come up, and I would not be in to work the next day. We needed to talk. I had just spent the money for our mortgage payment on bailing Dakota out of jail!

"I'm sorry," he started to say.

"Sorry isn't going to cut it this time! How are we going to pay for the mortgage?" I asked.

"We will figure it out. We always do." He replied, much calmer than I thought he should have been.

"That is enough!" I yelled, the dam of emotions finally bursting. "You need help! You're obviously still drunk and probably won't even remember what happened tomorrow! Don't think this is over, though!"

I was so mad that I couldn't stay at home. I planned on dropping Dakota off and heading out to my dad's for the night. I didn't bother grabbing any clothes or any supplies. I would just stay in my old room. I left the motor running and didn't bother to say anything to Dakota. As soon as Dakota got out of the truck, I turned around in the yard and headed back out of the driveway. I looked in my rearview mirror at Dakota standing there looking at my taillights. I wondered how long it would be before I had to pull out of this driveway permanently. At least I knew that he would have to sit at home and sober up while I was gone. His car was impounded. I had the truck and the keys to both cars.

I hit the gas hard, throwing rocks from the truck's rear tires as I pulled out onto the highway. I thought I heard a low, wicked-sounding laugh as I pulled away.

Sleepless nights were becoming the norm. The next day, I crawled out of my childhood bed and headed downstairs. Dad had already gone to work. He left me a fresh pot of coffee and a note wishing me good luck on a hard conversation that needed to be had. I used my dad's comb to go through my hair as best as I could, rinsed my mouth out with water, and quickly downed some coffee. I hadn't brought any clothing or grooming items with me. My appearance and coffee breath would match my mood.

The feeling I had driving home after leaving after a fight was becoming all too familiar. The happy love bubble that had led to our marriage was quickly becoming a memory. I arrived home. Dakota sat at the large wood table in the dining room, slouched over, drinking a cup of coffee. He looked equally as exhausted as I did. He eerily resembled the way he had looked the first night I had seen him with slightly too long, messy hair, a worn military-issue shirt, and gray sweatpants. I softened a bit at the memory.

He looked up and gave me a half-hearted smile, but it did not reach his eyes. "Hey," he said.

"Hey," I replied as I sat down across the table from him.

"Look, I'm going to just say this. You need help. I've known about your drinking for a while, but driving like that is a whole new level of stupid! Now, I have to come to your job not just to pick you up from work but to bail you out of jail!"

As if on cue, his phone rang, interrupting my rant. He looked down. "It's my supervisor," he said sadly. I sat quietly and listened to the short, mostly one-sided conversation. His shoulders sunk. "Yes, sir… I understand, sir…" The call was disconnected. Slowly, he looked up at me. "I just got fired." The anger that had begun to level out crept back.

"What did you expect? You work at the jail, and you just got arrested for driving drunk. Now, not only are we out the money for your bail, which should have paid our mortgage, but we have to find money for the fines and lawyer. Plus, you now have no income." I managed to keep my voice level, somehow. "Now, you don't have a choice. You will be forced by the court to go to counseling. We may also be forced to sell this damn farm, just like I suggested!" I slowly pulled my chair out, making a scraping sound. He sat with his face buried in his hands and said nothing. He knew I was right.

"Dear, I love you, but I can't talk about this anymore. I'm going to go out riding for a bit. I will be back later to make some food, but I need to be alone to think about what we can do. With that, I left him sitting alone at our table and headed to the barn to saddle Rampage. As I walked, I pulled my phone out of my pocket and dialed Celeste's number. She answered on the first ring but did not sound like herself. "Celeste, you're not going to believe what happened...." I went through the series of events that had occurred over the last few days.

Silence met me from the other line, which I thought was very strange coming from my best friend, especially considering what I had told her. Was I overburdening her with my problems? "Celeste? You there? Did I say something wrong?"

I heard her clear her throat, and her voice cracked as she said the following words. Words that broke my heart. "Solange, I have Cancer. It's Stage IV. That's why I have been feeling so crappy."

I didn't know what to say or how to react, which must have broken her heart in return.

Here I was, babbling about my problems and asking for her help, when it was she who needed me, for once.

A Few Months Later

Solange: Life felt like it was falling apart. Dakota and I were barely speaking. The money situation was getting dire. Dakota was serving 30 days in jail due to his drunk driving sentence. Celeste was going through treatments for her cancer, and I had lost my management job due to the business closing. It felt like my carefully built, perfect world was collapsing. I had found a job in the same field, but now I was only an assistant manager, not 'The' manager.

The pay was less, and without Dakota's income, we were drowning financially. My depression worsened. Some days, I felt like I was suffocating. I had my parents and a handful of other good friends. With Celeste going through Cancer treatments, I was trying to support her as best as I could while going through the hardest time I had, to date in my own life. I missed her, and really wished I could lean on her. I felt like such a lousy friend for even thinking that way.

I found myself feeling lost. I started just keeping to myself instead of talking to anyone. To make things worse, the dreams had returned. They came nightly now. I found myself waking, gasping for breath each night, in an empty bed, only Stryker and my kitty to keep me company. Worse yet, I couldn't remember what the dreams were about, only that the ghost woman and the ghost man were at the center of each one.

I was tired. I was angry. I didn't know what else to do but wait. With Dakota in jail, I wouldn't be able to make any decisions until his time was served. I really just wanted out, out of all of it. The feeling seemed to increase more each day.

I passed the days at work, hating the job and the lesser title. I spent the evenings cleaning the house and keeping up with the outdoor chores. I felt like I was trapped in a bad dream that repeated daily. With each passing day, I felt more lost, sad, and lonely.

Thanks to my parents, the hydrant in the tack room worked now, but the hole around it had never been filled in. It bothered me each time I saw it. After an exceptionally bad day at work, I decided to fill it in. I figured that some physical activity would help blow off some steam.

I fed and watered the horses and decided that I would need help. I immediately thought of my friend Lawrence. Both of my cars needed some work as well. I stopped showing them and was driving them less, with the farm becoming the priority. The cars mostly just sat now, which had caused them to deteriorate mechanically. Lawrence was great with old cars. If I called him, and he was able to spare some time to help out an old friend, I could kill two birds with one stone. Besides, some company would be nice. Maybe he could help to lift my spirits.

"Hey, Sol," he answered, using a nickname that only he was allowed to use. "What's up?"

"I need to ask a favor or two..." I replied. He gladly accepted my plea for help and said he was on his way. As stated, Lawrence showed up less than an hour after I called him.

Lawrence: As I pulled up to Sol's house, I wondered what was actually going on. She hadn't called or texted me since I had visited the farm for the last big party with our group of friends. Rumors had been flying within the group that there was some trouble in her marriage, but she had not reached out to anyone to talk about it if that were true. I chose not to pay much attention to the rumors. I had my own problems. My fiancé had recently left me. Supposedly, we 'grew apart,' but I knew there had been another man involved.

When I arrived, Sol was nowhere in sight. She had said she needed help with the cars, but more so, a hydrant in the barn. I didn't see her near the cars, so I parked my old SUV in the driveway and headed towards the barn. I had dressed in old, ripped jeans and an old work shirt so that I didn't need to be concerned about ruining clothes, no matter what we were doing. As I neared, I could hear what sounded like a shovel hitting dirt. I guessed she had already started the job.

"Sol, you in there?" I called so as not to scare her when I entered.

"Yep, in the tack room," she called.

Her appearance surprised me when I saw her. She was sweaty, and her face was streaked with dirt. That wasn't what caught me off guard. It was her eyes. She smiled when she saw me, but the smile didn't reach her eyes like it always had before. We had known each other since we were young, and something was definitely not right. It was like the light had faded from her eyes. She looked tired and somehow older, although it had not been that long since we had seen each other. I chose to keep the thought to myself and instead offered a hug.

"Thanks for coming," Solange said. "This hole has been here since my stepdad fixed the hydrant. My 'husband' just couldn't find the time to finish the job even though he's been unemployed for a while now."

A bit of spark seemed to show back up in her eyes as she spoke. I cocked my head to the side to show her that I was listening. She seemed like she needed a listening ear more than she needed help filling the hole or working on her cars. I made a mental note to find more reasons to call or text her. Maybe even find a few more reasons to stop by.

Solange threw me a shovel, and I joined her, throwing dirt back into the hole. I let her continue to tell me about everything that had recently happened, occasionally interjecting an opinion to let her know I was listening. She really had needed someone to talk to, and I was realizing that it was doing me equally as much good to be that friend.

Suddenly, my shovel hit something that was not dirt with a loud 'tink' sound. We both stopped for a moment. Solange's mouth formed a surprised 'O'.

Solange: It felt good and so natural to talk to Lawrence. Once I started, it felt like I couldn't stop. I hadn't realized how much I had bottled up and how much I really needed to talk to someone about it. Our conversation was interrupted by a loud 'tink' sound like metal hitting metal as Lawrence's shovel hit something that was not dirt.

The sound unexpectedly jogged a memory. I had heard the same sound when Waylon was digging the hole but had completely forgotten about it due to Dakota's arrival that day. "Stop," I said. "I think you hit something metal." We both put down our shovels and kneeled next to the pile of dirt, beginning to dig with our hands. As we searched, I began to feel a familiar sick feeling creeping into my stomach and a vision-blurring headache forming in the back of my eyes.

"You ok, Solange?" Lawrence asked, his eyes filled with concern.

"Just a little headache. I'm probably a little dehydrated," I replied. About that time, our hands connected with something. It felt cold and solid. We pulled it out together. It appeared to be a very rusty box.

"That's a really weird thing to be buried in a barn," Lawrence said.

My head was pounding, and my sight was getting increasingly blurred by the moment, but even the pain could not stop my curiosity. Lawrence brushed the clay off the box. It was clearly a lock box, but it looked like the entire thing was about to fall apart.

"Try hitting the front of it with your shovel to see if it will come open. I want to see what's in that box," I told Lawrence. He looked back at me, about to question my request. I grabbed my temple as a shooting pain invaded my head. "Just do it!" I said, trying not to grit my teeth.

Lawrence stood and raised the shovel above his head, bringing it down on the front of the box with all his might. I thought I heard a male voice scream, "Nooo!" At the same time as the shovel hit the front of the box, another pain shot through my skull, this time causing me to pass out...

A short time later...

I came to on the couch in the house with a cold rag on my forehead and Lawrence sitting on a chair in front of me, looking very concerned. I blinked a couple of times, realizing the headache and stomachache were mostly gone.

"You're awake!" Lawrence said, leaning forward, a lock of his long, curly hair falling over one eye.

I smiled at him. "How did I get in the house?" I asked.

He smiled back. "I carried you."

I couldn't help but notice how attractive my long-time friend was.

"I'm sorry. I didn't mean to scare you. I get bad headaches that knock me out like this every once in a while," I said.

"I just got you up here. If you would have stayed out, I was going to call 911," he said, his forehead creased with concern.

"I'm ok, I promise. Just a migraine," I said. Suddenly, I remembered the box. "Lawrence, did you get the box open?" I asked.

"Ya, it popped open." He shook his head as if he didn't understand the question.

"Well, where is it?" I asked, sitting up quickly, causing another wave of pain in my head.

"Umm, I kinda forgot about it when you passed out. Why is it so important?" he asked, looking confused.

"Because I have a feeling," I said, squinting my eyes at him. "Can you go get it? I really want to see what is in it."

"Sure." He took off, heading for the door. He soon returned carrying the box. As he did, the headache increased in intensity more than ever before. I fought to fend off the feeling of passing out, and this time I won. He placed the rusty, now broken box on the coffee table in front of the couch where I had been lying.

"Do you want me to open it, or do you want to open it," he asked, a mischievous glint taking over his features.

"You go ahead," I said nervously.

He placed one hand on the bottom of the box to steady it and one on the now broken top. Slowly and carefully, he separated the two portions of the box. He placed the top of the box upside down on the table next to the bottom. We both leaned forward, knocking our heads in the process. We pulled back, rubbed our foreheads where they had bumped and giggled.

"OK, you opened the box. I get to see what's in it first," I said. Once again, I leaned forward. This time, Lawrence waited.

Inside the box were what looked to be the very de-teriorated remains of a very old gun and some scraps of yellowed paper. I reached for the paper first. It im-mediately crumbled, beyond repair, upon my touch. I reached for what was left of the gun, leaving the scraps of deteriorated paper where they were. I word-lessly handed the rusted piece of metal resembling a gun to Lawrence.

"What in the world?" His words trailed off.

"Lawrence, we need to put this back in the box and take it to the police tomorrow. It's too late tonight, and it's not an emergency, so I don't think we should bring it in right now. I want you to stay here in the spare bedroom tonight so we can go in together tomorrow," I said.

We woke up early the following day and placed the box containing the gun and paper remnants into a large bag. After coffee, we headed to town in my pickup, with the bag placed carefully in the back seat. We drove to town and then to the police station. The receptionist greeted us, asking if we were there to visit Dakota. I explained that we needed to speak to the Sheriff. Lawrence held on to the bag. We were ush-ered into the office and sat waiting to visit with the sheriff.

The Sheriff, a middle-aged, heavy-set man with thick black hair and a uniform that barely fit, leaned back heavily on his chair, causing it to groan as if in pain. He looked almost bored as we presented him with the bag containing our found treasure.

"So, you found this in a pile of dirt that was dug out around the fire hydrant in your barn?" He questioned.

"Yes, sir. That is correct," I confirmed. I relayed the details of the events as best as I could remember them. Lawrence sat fidgeting nervously next to me. He was clearly uncomfortable. The sheriff glanced his way suspiciously several times. He never spoke to him, however.

"Well, in this condition, there won't be much we can do to find evidence. We can send the gun and what's left of the paper off for testing. I can look into the history of the place where you live. This will take some time. You will hear back from me as soon as I know anything.

Lawrence nervously spoke. "Solange, what about what the realtor told you and Dakota when you moved in?"

The Sheriff scowled at Lawrence. "Mrs. Ogden, what is this 'young gentleman' talking about?"

"Are you from around here, Sir?" I asked.

"No, I've only been in the area for a few years. I moved from out of state," he replied.

"OK, well, the realtor told Dakota and me that the original owners of the place died out there."

He cocked his head, now seeming interested. "I will have to look into that to see if there is any truth to it, and if so, if these items could be related." With that, he dismissed us. Lawrence breathed an audible sigh as we left the room.

"Did you see the way he kept looking at me? It's like he wanted to find a reason to arrest me just because I have long hair. I may or may not have done some things when I was a kid, but that doesn't make me a criminal now," he said, only half joking. Some of the nervousness had left now that we were out of the Sheriff's office.

We decided to visit Dakota while we were in the same building as the jail. I checked my watch, and we were still within visiting hours. It would be another couple of weeks before he finished his jail time.

Dakota smiled as he was escorted around the corner to the visiting area and saw me. The smile quickly dropped when he saw Lawrence by my side. I couldn't read his expression. "Hey, Solange. Hey, Lawrence." His gritted teeth as he said Lawrence's name. "What are you doing here?" He shot Lawrence a sideways glance as he asked.

I looked back and forth between the men. Tension filled the room. "Well, I asked Lawrence to help me fill in the hole in the barn where we fixed the hydrant. While we were shoveling the dirt back into the hole, we found something. Something we had to bring here."

"What?" Dakota asked, with his full attention now on me.

"A very old lock box with a gun and what looked to be some sort of note in it," I replied.

Dakota's eyes flashed for a moment with what I could have sworn was alarm. He quickly changed the subject. "What the hell is 'he' doing out there 'helping' you when you're out there alone?" He directed an angry stare at Lawrence. "You trying to steal my wife while I'm stuck in here, boy?" Dakota stood up quickly, hands on the table, shoving the chair backward with a loud scraping sound. This attracted the attention of the guard.

"Whoa, I'm just trying to help Sol. She called me asking for help with her cars and filling in that hole." Though he was still seated, and his tone was calm, his eyes challenged Dakota.

At that moment, a young guard, rivaling Dakota in size, strode over to our table. Apparently, we had drawn the attention of almost everyone in the room as it had gone silent. "Is there a problem over here?" the guard asked in a deep voice.

"Ya, this 'friend' of ours has been spending time alone with my wife while I'm in here!" Dakota growled.

"OK, visiting time is over." The guard said as he led Dakota away, scowling back at us the entire time. Lawrence looked annoyed as we left the building.

"I'm sorry, I don't know what's gotten into him lately." I apologized to Lawrence.

Lawrence: Now I knew why the light appeared to be gone from Sol's eyes. That jerk was treating her like dirt! Maybe even hurting her. It was hard to tell, and she wasn't ready to tell anyone if that was the case. He wasn't going to stop me from being around her. She had asked me for my help, and it was clear she was exhausted and in need of a friend. I was going to be that friend whether her jerk of a husband wanted me to or not.

Solange: The next couple of weeks went by quickly. I had not heard back from the Sheriff. The dreams increased in frequency but not in clarity. Lawrence and I finished filling in the hole near the hydrant. He also started work on both cars. Life sped by quickly. I had not visited Dakota again since he had been so surly the last time. I found the fact that life seemed better without him at home and that I barely missed him a bit disturbing.

The evening before he was to return home, I received the call back from the Sheriff. "Mrs. Ogden, as we suspected, we weren't able to find any evidence from the gun. The paper scraps fell apart even more when we tried to test them. What I can tell you is that both the paper and the gun date back to the late 1920s and early 1930s. I can also confirm that the original owner of the farm and his wife were shot and killed on the farm. What's left of the gun you brought in may or may not be the murder weapon. It's too deteriorated to tell exactly what it was."

I listened carefully. A feeling of fear suddenly settled over me.

"From what we can tell from historical records, the killer was never found. The hired man found them and reported their deaths to the law."

The conversation was short and to the point. I thanked the Sheriff for his time. I would be picking Dakota up the next morning, along with the lockbox and its contents. The conversation had exhausted me. Though it was early, I went to bed. I knew it was going to be a long day bringing Dakota home. The bills were piling up with the loss of his income and the addition of his legal bills. I still loved him, but would that love be enough to keep us together with all the challenges facing us?

I laid my head down on my pillow, thinking about the past few years since Dakota and I had gotten together. I had a paid-off home, two nice cars, a pickup, no debt, and a ton of friends before we decided to buy this place. Now, I had lost my management job, which I had worked so hard to put myself through college to earn. Dakota had lost his job. My cars were slowly deteriorating, bills were behind and getting more so by the day, and my best friend was dying of Cancer. This place had to be cursed...

Dakota Comes Home

Solange: The ride home was silent. I had no idea where to even start with Dakota. Each time I glanced his way, he was staring blankly out the window. How do you address a failing marriage? He had said no to further counseling. He said that he would look for work, but what was there for a man who had just lost his license and now had a criminal record?

The following days passed in much the same way. I went to and from my job. Now, I was the only one earning a paycheck. Dakota seemed to be distancing himself further and further. We didn't even sleep in the same bed anymore. When I came home each evening, I would find him in the same place I left him: on the couch, TV on, and laptop open in his lap. He would tell me that he was looking for a job, but every time I would attempt to look at the screen of his computer, he would snap it closed and, worse yet, snap at me in short outbursts. Just enough to make me want to stop asking.

His appearance changed as well. He allowed his hair to grow out and, much of the time, skipped showering, so it was often greasy and, even when clean, went uncombed. Instead of his usually neat, kept goatee, he grew a large, bushy beard that I hated. With the lack of activity, he put on weight as well. I felt that with the change in his appearance, the difference in our age became more apparent.

Though he was home all the time and not working, the housework still seemed to fall only on me, as well as the cooking and laundry. I was miserable. The bills were at the point of final notice being received. There were no potential job offers or even interviews for Dakota. My world seemed to be falling apart. I wondered if others could tell from the outside looking in. I couldn't take another job to bring in more money, or there would be no one to take care of the farm and animals or to keep us fed.

I was exhausted and didn't know what else to do. I hadn't seen or talked to any of my friends in such a long time that I couldn't remember when the last time was. Even conversations with my parents had become few and far between. Life felt like it had become a never-ending cycle of work. I worked a job that wasn't earning enough money to pay the bills. I worked to try to keep my home presentable: meals made, animals cared for, and clean clothes for us to wear. I worked to try to keep a failing relationship afloat. Each day, I felt myself falling deeper into depression.

One evening, on my drive home, my phone rang in my pocket. I pulled it out and smiled. It was Lawrence. "Hey," I answered.

"Hey, it's Lawrence," he said dryly.

"I know who it is. These new-fangled things, called cell phones, do have caller IDs. You ever heard of it?" I joked.

He laughed a little on the other line. His refusal to get a smartphone had been a running joke between us for a long time. "I haven't heard from you in a while. Just wondering how you and…. Dakota… are doing?" He hesitated a bit as he said Dakota's name. "Did you ever find anything out about the gun and box?"

I went silent for a moment. I had forgotten about it with everything else going on.

"Hello? You still there?" His voice snapped me back to reality.

"Sorry, Lawrence, I completely forgot about it. There's been a lot going on. The Sheriff returned the box, and I brought it back when I picked up Dakota. They weren't able to find anything out about it with the age and deterioration. The Sheriff did confirm that there had been a murder on the farm many years ago, but that's about all I know. I think the box is still in the backseat of my truck."

"Are you free to get together?" he asked. "I have been doing some research." I could almost see his hopeful face as he spoke.

I pulled the truck over, thinking about what I had to look forward to at home, and made a quick decision. "OK, let's grab some food in town," I said.

For the first time in a while, I felt a spark of excitement. I quickly sent a text to Dakota and decided I would bring him some food home instead of cooking for once. The splurge would be worth it. I turned the truck around and headed back to town to see my friend. A real smile graced my face for the first time in a very long time.

A short time later, I found myself sitting across a booth from Lawrence, beer in hand, a bacon cheeseburger with grilled mushroom and onions, and a gooey order of cheese balls in front of me. I smiled and felt relaxed as the first mouth-watering bite hit my taste buds. Lawrence had not touched his own food. He looked concerned.

"This is sooo good! I can't tell you how much I needed this..." I took a few more bites, then paused, noticing that Lawrence still had not touched his food. "What's wrong?" I asked.

"Well, I wanted to tell you what I found out when I looked into the past of your farm and that gun, but from the look of you, I think you need a friend. What's really going on out there?" He asked.

I thought about his words for a moment. I realized that I was still wearing my red uniform top. I hadn't looked at my hair or makeup in hours, and I hadn't slept well in a very long time between the dreams and the stress. I hadn't thought about checking my appearance in my excitement before going to meet Lawrence. I put my burger down and patted my hair, feeling a bit self-conscious now. I should have known he would notice once he saw me. I pinched the bridge of my nose and exhaled sharply. I proceeded to spill my guts about what had been going on at home. Lawrence listened with concern in his eyes.

"Wow, that's a lot," he said as I finished. "Why didn't you say something?"

"Look, I told you. Now, can we just talk about something else? I came here to get my mind off of all of that, not talk about it more." I felt close to tears. It felt good to tell someone, but it also made me realize how much I had been holding in.

He looked like he wanted to say something, but he didn't. Instead, he took a bite of his own burger and chewed slowly before speaking again. "OK, don't think I'm dropping this, but we will talk about something else for the moment," he said.

I gave him a relieved smile. "Thanks," I said. We finished our meals, and each ordered a second beer.

"I went to the library after we found the gun. I looked at the public records and newspapers from back in the late 20s to early 30s in this area. I found something." Lawrence's tone became very serious as he spoke. "The realtor was telling the truth. This farm really was sold off piece by piece by its original owners. Their names were Cecil and Matilda Amos. They were a young married couple, a lot like you and Dakota. They are the ones who were murdered there. The farmhand found them and made the police report. The murder weapon was never found, and no arrest was ever made. It was assumed to have been a drifter looking for something to steal as times were hard back then." His brows furrowed as he finished the story.

I was very intrigued, though most of the information was what the Sheriff had relayed, just in more detail. "You don't look convinced," I said.

"I'm not," he continued. "I can't put my finger on it, but something about it doesn't add up. Plus, it gets even more stranger from there. The piece of the farm that is your place now has changed hands every few years since then. Always to married couples of varying ages. There have been numerous accidents out there. Basically, by searching the ownership records, death records, and newspaper clips, it looks to me like every owner of your place, as well as anyone who has tried to help out there, has had something bad happen to them."

My eyes widened, and my jaw dropped. I thought about how happy Dakota and I had been and how things were now. I thought about my best friend's health and how she had been trying to warn me. I also thought about the conversation with the old farmer who had formerly owned the place.

"Lawrence, this can't all be a coincidence. We need to sell that place! Lawrence, you need to stay away from me and stop looking into this anymore before you end up having something bad happen to you, too. Celeste tried to help by helping me get rid of the piano, and now, look what has happened to her."

"I have a theory…" He started before I could object further. I think the original owners have stayed on that farm for some reason. I think it has something to do with their deaths, and they haven't let anyone else live 'happily ever after' out there because of whatever happened."

"Stop." I all but shouted, putting my finger over his lips from across the table to shush him. "I couldn't bear it if something happened to you too." My eyes welled with tears. "Please stop…. For me… My life is already falling apart. Let me figure this out on my own and stay away from me for a while…for your own good." With that, I could no longer hold back the tears. I threw a twenty-dollar bill on the table, turned on my heel, and left Lawrence sitting alone at the table, stunned.

As I stormed towards my truck, I remembered that I had forgotten to order food for Dakota. It was late, and I was tired. Exhausted, really. The talk with Lawrence had left me even more drained. I decided just to grab something at a drive-thru for Dakota and head home for an early bedtime.

I arrived home with a bag of food. Dakota was parked on the couch playing a video game, exactly where he had been when I had left that morning. He propped himself up on an elbow. "Did you have fun with your little friend?" he said, with an edge to his voice and a now familiar mean glint in his eyes.

"Argh..." I groaned. "I'm not in the mood to argue with you tonight, Dakota. All I have been doing for what seems like forever is working. I think I deserved a bit of a break." I dropped the bag of food in front of him and headed up the stairs to our bedroom, knowing I would be spending yet another night alone in our bed with only my dog and cat for company.

Feeling Defeated

Solange: I had tried everything to make our marriage work. I had tried talking about our problems and expressing how I was feeling. I had tried fighting back. I had tried the silent treatment. I had even suggested counseling, which he had refused. Everything had just seemed to spin out of control. Finally, I felt defeated.

The fighting was almost constant now. He just seemed constantly angry. When he wasn't sleeping, he was playing video games or watching TV. We never touched each other anymore, and to my surprise, he hadn't even noticed when I had stopped wearing my wedding band.

If I were being honest with myself, I would have known that my marriage was over for a long time. I had just been too stubborn to stop trying for a way to save us. We had said our vows in front of God, friends, and family. I had taken those vows very seriously. I wasn't about to give up without a fight.

Feeling like a maid most of the time and invisible the rest was one thing. Walking on eggshells in my own home, in fear of somehow causing a fight all the time, was unbearable. I spent most of my time cooking and trying to keep up with cleaning up after him. I was also working a dead-end job that I hated, as the business where I had gotten my first Management job after graduating college had closed its doors. I could have handled it if only I felt there was a reason to hold on.

I did my best to be a good wife. I just brushed off feeling unloved, but the fighting, in addition to the rest of life's stresses, was getting to be too much. Between work and my failing marriage, I felt trapped. Happiness had begun to feel like a made-up concept.

The Mystery Begins to Unravel

Solange: I wasn't asleep long before the dreams started. They were now a part of each night. This time, it was different. This time, like the very first dream I had about the farmer and his wife, it seemed real. I was still on the farm. I was near the grove, and I was not alone. I found myself watching a horrific scene unfold. I tried to call out to warn her, but I had no voice.

She was chained to a tree. I could hear her pleading. Her hands above her head were raw and bleeding. Her legs buckled and no longer supported her weight. Tears streamed down her dirty, bruised face. His face contorted into a wicked smile. I heard his maniacal laughter as he ignored her pleas for mercy.

"This is all your fault. You convinced me to come out here. I had it all. I would have been inheriting my father's business by now. Instead, I am out here in the dirty, God-forsaken prairie, working my hands to the bone like I never have before in all my life, and still failing! All because you wanted a farm!" I could hear the anger in his words.

"Please, Cecil!" I heard her cry. "Please don't hurt me more. We can sell the rest and move back east. I'm sure your parents would still have a job for you. I can cook and clean for whoever needs the help."

"You don't understand. It doesn't matter how much we sell. We are so far in debt that this place and everything on it is about to be taken by the bank." With that, he drew a small revolver from behind his back and shot her. I saw her body go limp.

As if magically, I was face to face with Amos, but he did not seem able to see me. I saw him withdraw a sheet of paper from his pocket. I was able to read it.

"To whoever finds this:
I'm sorry for what I have done.
I could no longer take care of my family.
I need it to end.
This is the only way I know how.
Now, the property can be someone else's dream without me losing it,

-Cecil Amos"

I screamed. Once again, no sound came out of my mouth. I tried to grab his arm, but my hand went right through it. He put the gun in his mouth and pulled the trigger. The note remained gripped in his hand as he fell heavily to the ground.

Then, once again, the scene changed as if someone had hit the fast-forward button on a movie. I stood in the same spot as a rusted old farm truck rolled into the driveway, skidding to an abrupt halt as the driver spotted the bodies. The wife was still hanging from the tree. Her hands were still chained, lock holding the chain to the tree. The farmer lay not far from her body, gun in one hand, the scrap of paper in the other.

He parked the truck, frozen by the scene he had just driven up to. He had just been coming to do his chores. There were a lot of chores to do now, as he was the only farm hand left working for the failing farm. He was arriving early just as the sun was rising. Now, he was facing what appeared to be a murder or suicide scene.

He appeared to be contemplating his next move. After quite some time, he exited the old truck and slowly walked up to the scene. He kicked the gun out of the hand of the dead man. He slowly knelt next to the farmer and took the scrap of paper from his hand, reading it carefully. The look on his face went from blank to shocked. Then, it appeared that he had a moment of clarity.

"OK, boss, one more favor," he muttered quietly. "We can't have folks knowing what you did." He rifled through the farmer's overall pocket, finding a key ring. He tried several keys in the lock until he found the one that matched the lock that attached the chain to the tree holding the poor farmer's wife. He allowed her body to slump over his shoulder and carried her body into the house. The large farmhand then hefted the farmer's body over his shoulder like a sack of potatoes and carried him into the house. I followed him into the house, apparently still unable to be seen or heard.

The farmhand had placed the sprawled body of the farmwife in the kitchen, and the farmer in the doorway positioned as if he were trying to get to his wife. He then proceeded to ransack the house. He found a lockbox containing a small amount of cash, stuffed the cash in his pocket, and placed the lockbox under his arm.

He headed back out to the tree line and placed the gun and note in the lockbox. He then relocked the lock that had previously held the farmwife and hid the lock and chain amongst the tree branches, making it all but invisible. He carefully kicked dirt and leaves around the area where blood had saturated the ground where the farmer and his wife had died, hiding the scene the rest of the way. He locked the lockbox and placed the key in his pocket. He sat the box on the seat of his old truck and drove down to the barn.

I watched as he went over to where the hydrant we had recently repaired was, dug a hole around it, and then buried the lockbox. Then, he did the chores as if nothing had happened. He drove away. I was still standing in the barn when I heard another vehicle pull into the yard. I walked back out into the yard and saw the old truck returning, followed by a sheriff's car. The farmhand exited the truck and pointed to the house.

Then I was back in my room again. I was still not alone. The woman whose murder I had just witnessed stood beside my bed. I backpedaled in the bed, making myself as small as I could against the headboard.

"Shhh... I'm here. I'm real. I'm not going to hurt you," she said in a soft, sweet voice.

For some reason, I was no longer afraid. "Who are you?" I asked, my voice barely a whisper.

Her eyes lit up. "I can't believe you can see me... or hear me! I have been trapped here for so long..." Her voice trailed off.

"What... do you mean?" I asked, now confused, as to if I was asleep or awake and if this was real.

"I am... or was... Matilda Amos. My husband and I built this house and used to own all the farmland around it as well. I have been trapped here since I died," she said.

"Why can I see you?" I asked.

"I am not sure," she replied. "I have tried to get help from the others who have lived here over the years and have only succeeded in scaring them away. Cecil is much more powerful than me. Here, let me show you." Before I could say anything, she touched a single finger to the side of my temple. Images of a series of families passed before my eyes as if I were watching a movie.

"These are all the families that have lived here since I died. When Cecil killed us, for some reason, it trapped us here. I have been trying to get someone to help me since then. Cecil enjoys it. He gets meaner each year," she said sadly.

As she showed me, I could feel the sadness coming from her. It seemed that the tragedies and anger got worse as each generation passed. Divorces, injuries, sickness, and even death. I was horrified. At one point, she showed me the old bent-over farmer I had met and his wife. She was the closest to communicating with Matilda, but then she had gotten cancer - just like my best friend.

Lastly, she showed me how Dakota and I had looked through her eyes from when we moved in until now. I could see Cecil, and I could see him putting words into Dakota's head.... Influencing him to do the things he had been doing. Trying to turn Dakota into... him... I gasped. "Why are you showing me this? What do you want from me?" I wailed, all the recent pain hitting me all at once.

"Because I need your help," she said quietly. "I think the only way for us to leave is to destroy the thing that bound my physical body. The lock that latched the chain that bound me to the tree where I died. Each time you have changed or destroyed something that was a piece of us, you have weakened him and strengthened me. That lock is the last thing left untouched."

With that, she pointed to the grove, and then she was gone. I blinked. I was in my bed. I was not backed up against the headboard, and I was alone in the room. I took a deep breath and shook my head. I was wide awake now. *Was that real or a dream?*

I got up and showered, deeply bothered by what had just happened. I thought back to seeing the rusted old lock in the tree when I was with Celeste and Lawrence. I remembered how sick I had gotten. I remembered the other times I had similar experiences. Dreams, dizzy spells… it all added up now. It had been Matilda trying to warn me and ultimately save me from a similar fate to hers.

The tree grove, the hay loft, the piano, the gun, they all tied together the story of a life cut too short by a very angry man. Not just her life but the curse put on the place and the many other ruined lives that followed. Now, she had found her voice again after all of these years. She found me. She needed my help.

How Could I Escape?

Solange: I knew what needed to be done. First, to convince Dakota to sell our beloved farm. Then, to somehow destroy the lock. I had to figure out if there was anything left of Dakota and I's marriage to try to save.

As the warm water steamed over my body, I closed my eyes. I formulated a plan. I was going to spring the sale of the farm on Dakota after I got off work. I would cite the increasing amount of bills as the reason.

Work went by slowly. I knew I was just going through the motions to get the day done. At least it was a busy day, which made things go quicker. A few favorite customers came in, making the day tolerable. By the end of the day, I was nervous but ready to present my idea to Dakota.

I finished the day, locked the store, and headed home, rehearsing what I would say to Dakota the whole way. I decided to make some supper first and hoped that a meal together would soften the blow.

When I got home, as usual, he was sitting on the couch exactly where I left him. I pasted a smile on my face and greeted him. "Hey, hun," I said cheerfully.

He turned his head away from the TV, a frown appearing on his face. "Why are you so cheery?" He growled.

"Got to see a few of my favorite customers today. I gained a couple of new customers to up my numbers. Just a good day. I thought I'd make some chicken bacon ranch sandwiches and tater tots, and we could eat supper together." I smiled convincingly at him.

"Um, OK..." he said. His confusion was apparent from his face and the tone of his voice.

I busied myself trying to tidy up the kitchen, which had become a disaster with Dakota home all the time and me working so much. Then I set to work making a favorite meal. The smell filled the house, and I must have softened Dakota's mood.

He was smiling for the first time I could remember in a long time as I entered the living room with two hot plates of food. I moved some clutter off the coffee table, trying not to show my disgust, and sat the food down. I sat down beside him on my now filthy-stained couch, a smile still pasted on my face.

"I hope you like it," I said cheerily.

I reached for the remote and shut off the TV. His smile faded, but he didn't say anything. Instead, he picked up a sandwich and took a large bite. We finished our meal in silence. He wiped his face with the back of his hand, then sat back, a hand on his stomach, releasing a happy sigh. I cleared the plates and put them in the dishwasher, then came back and sat next to him on the couch. I waited a moment before I spoke.

"Dakota, I need to talk to you," I said.

He groaned in displeasure. "I knew you making supper and being so cheery was too good to be true."

I could no longer hold my composure. "Dakota... we have got to sell this place before we lose it. We're drowning in debt, and look what it has done to us..." I threw my arms around his broad shoulders, letting the tears I had held back for so many months flow freely. To my surprise, he stiffened at my touch. I pulled back and looked at him through tear-filled eyes.

Anger seemed to radiate from every cell of his body. His eyes appeared glossy. "I will die before I sell this place or let someone take it from me!" He yelled.

I knew then that it was already too late...

The Final Straw

Solange: I had left four times before, but this time was it. Anger and disappointment filled my heart. I had finally made up my mind. I was done.

A bad blizzard was forecasted, so I drove into town to stay with a friend. The road to 13 Mile Farm was paved but not a priority for plowing, making travel after a blizzard very difficult at times.

I was the Assistant Manager at the store where I worked and was the only one scheduled to work, so I had to be there. Though I knew there was no chance for upward momentum at the job, I still did my best to do what was expected of me. If nothing else, I at least knew for myself that I was doing the right thing.

When I told Dakota I would stay with my friend, he hadn't even objected to me leaving. Little did he know that this was a test. I wanted to see what his reaction to me being gone for a few days would be. Would I be missed, or would his behavior and actions remain the same no matter what I did?

My mom, Charlotte, had been my confidant throughout the last few years. She knew how hard I had been trying. She also knew that I was at a breaking point. I felt my back was against a wall, so we formulated a plan. I was going to go to work as scheduled. Once I was done at work, she was to meet me at the local lawyer's office.

I had been a nervous wreck all day, thinking about what must be done. My time at work drug by. It had been a slow day due to the blizzard just clearing, and I hadn't seen many customers. My stomach churned as I finished my workday, locked the door, and set the alarm. I headed toward what would become a pivotal moment in my life.

Though it was only a short drive between my work and the lawyer's office downtown, it seemed to take hours. The closer I got to the office, the more real the task ahead of me became. I felt nervous and scared. My reaction mirrored my emotions as I pulled into the parking lot and parked in front of the bland brick building with white trim that was the lawyer's office.

The inner turmoil I had felt all day reached my eyes, and then the tears came. To my relief, my mom's car was already in the parking lot. I could see her tall, lean frame leaning against the building, waiting for me, messing with a string of her long blonde hair. I knew her support would help me get through what was sure to be a painful task.

I was silent as I exited my pickup and walked towards the office's cold, uninviting metal door. Thoughts thundered through my mind. *Pull yourself together. You know what must be done.*

I took a deep breath and wiped my eyes. My mom saw the tears and reacted immediately. She pushed away from the building where she had been leaning, waiting for me. She wrapped her arms around me in an empathetic hug.

"Dad is never going to speak to me again," I said in anguish as my lip started to quiver. My mom understood. She and my dad had divorced several years ago.

"He will get over it," she said calmly. "You are here to do what is best for you. Now, are you sure this is it?"

I broke away from her hug, wiped my eyes again, and shook my head yes. I still felt a bit unsure, but better with my mom's reassurance. I stood up straight, squared my shoulders, and we walked into the lawyer's office, my mom holding my hand.

To my surprise, I was able to keep a straight face and avoid breaking down as I explained my situation to the lawyer. He emotionlessly explained my options. He was all business, seemingly not at all empathetic to my situation and the pain it was causing me. I didn't like him, but I could tell he was the right man to handle the job. There would be no negotiating with him once things were in writing. Everything would go as was written in the papers with fairness to both Dakota and me.

After about an hour of listening to the lawyer drone on about the specifics of the divorce and asking me a multitude of questions, the painful initial meeting was done. I handed him a check for the deposit and had the primary paperwork for a divorce in my hands.

Before leaving the office, the lawyer stopped me. "Mrs. Ogden, you don't have to serve your husband the papers. If you change your mind, and nothing is received back within 30 days, nothing further will happen, and the paperwork will be void." For a moment, he seemed almost sympathetic.

I managed to hold my chin up and paste on a fake smile. The words stung, and momentarily, I began to doubt what I had just done. "Thank you, sir. I appreciate your assistance with this matter and all the information you have provided," I said in my most professional voice.

My mom and I left the office. We stopped for a moment outside the office. I exhaled a sigh, allowed my shoulders to relax, and the fake smile fell off my face. Now that I had the paperwork, it would be up to me to decide if I would deliver it to Dakota.

"Do you want me to return to the farm with you?" My mom asked with concern.

"No thanks, Mom. I appreciate you, but this is something I need to do on my own." Despite my best effort, as I finished the sentence, a tear escaped my eyes. For a moment, as I looked at her, she appeared younger. It was like I was looking at a mirrored image of myself.

"I have been there. I understand how this feels. Please call me if you need anything," Mom said with a sad smile.

"Thank you for always being there," I said as I hugged her. I could only imagine how much worse this could have been without my mother to lean on. Then, I crawled into my truck to head home—the drive home drug by. The divorce papers felt heavy in my coat pocket. I drove a bit slower, partially due to the snow but mostly due to the desire to put off the inevitable.

I made it to the driveway and was immediately faced with an obstacle. Dakota hadn't taken the time to plow the large drift from the mouth of the driveway. It was still impassable after the blizzard. I texted him so he knew I would be home this evening. Evidently, the thought of me not being able to get in had not crossed his mind, or worse yet, had not mattered to him. This was already not starting off well.

As had become the norm, it appeared that I would have to take care of the situation myself. I backed my truck up, put it in four high, and charged the driveway entrance. A loud crash joined the rumble of the dual exhaust of my truck as snow exploded from the drift. I hit the brakes and came to a sliding halt. I came inches away from hitting Dakota's car! He had parked it near the end of the driveway so that he could get out if he needed to without plowing—sheer selfishness and laziness. I shut the truck off and walked the rest of the way down the driveway to the house, already annoyed.

The house was dark other than the glow from the TV. I knew he had heard my truck crash through the drift in the driveway. He hadn't even bothered to move off the couch. I tried to wipe the annoyed look from my face and speak calmly. "Hi," I said coldly.

He barely moved. He lifted his head slightly and looked at me lazily. "Did you bring me food?" Dakota asked.

"No...," I replied, trying to keep my cool.

"I suppose you aren't going to make any either." He rolled his eyes, laid his head back down on the pillow, and turned his attention back to the TV.

Now I was furious. "Really?!?! I'm gone for three days, and that's all you can say. No, welcome home; I missed you. All you want is food?" I asked through gritted teeth.

He looked up as if bored. "Are we really going to do this again?"

I just shook my head and groaned in frustration. He then proceeded to get up off the couch, grabbed his soda, and headed upstairs. I stood frozen for a moment. His selfishness and his lack of care totally took me aback. His actions and attitude had just made my decision easy.

I looked around at my disgusting, dirty home. After only three days of being gone, trash was everywhere, including overflowing around the garbage can. The cat boxes were stinky and full, and dirty dishes were stacked everywhere. I was really glad that no one other than Dakota and I had seen this mess. The house I loved so much actually stunk. I was embarrassed that it had come to this. Instead of a place of peace, my home had become comparable to my own personal prison.

I set to work cleaning. After several hours of work, the house was presentable and no longer stunk. Anger built, about to come to a boiling point as I set to work, making a huge batch of his favorite meal. Now he had the food he had requested and a presentable house again. I could do what had to be done without feeling guilty about leaving him unfed and in a messy house, at least. Lastly, I laid the divorce papers on the kitchen table. I looked down at them with a heavy sigh as I walked away.

I felt numb. So many emotions were present that I couldn't identify what they were. I went upstairs and walked into our bedroom, where he lay on the bed watching TV. He didn't move. "The house is clean, and dinner is made," I stated coldly. "And there are divorce papers on the table that I need you to sign. I'm leaving." Finally, I got his attention.

"What?!?!" he said quietly as he sat up.

"I'm leaving," I repeated. "I'm done!" I grabbed a cardboard box and started shoving essential items into it.

His demeanor had changed from uncaring and bored to seemingly devastated in the blink of an eye.

"But I still love you," he said.

I knew I had caught him off guard. I also knew he was taking me seriously now. Tears silently began to flow from his eyes. Unfortunately, this shook me. I allowed him to hug me, and I hugged him back. I was angry and hurt but not heartless. I had steeled myself while cleaning, but this was still much more difficult than I had thought it would be while I was angry. I hated the mix of feelings that I was having.

"Don't go," Dakota said in a quiet voice.

"I have to. This has happened too many times."

I regained my composure, the fact that his actions had spoken much louder than his words resurfacing in my mind. I grabbed the cardboard box filled with my stuff and left him standing there. I took my cat and dog and headed for the door before I could change my mind. I knew I was doing the right thing, but that did not make it hurt any less. *How did we get here when we were so happy?* I thought to myself as I drove away, tears streaming down my cheeks.

The End of Our Story

Solange: When I left the house, I knew I would never walk through the door as his wife again. I was closing a chapter. This was no longer my home... I moved away, back to my old trailer house. I took my name off all the bills at the farm and gave up my rights to the property in the divorce.

Inevitably, Dakota lost the farm due to non-payment. From what I heard, he had to be escorted off the property.

I started seeing Lawrence, not just as a friend, but now as a boyfriend. Life seemed to be improving. I had not forgotten about my encounter with Matilda, though the dreams had stopped after I moved away from the farm. A lingering feeling of guilt stayed with me. I knew I needed to do something. The farm was scheduled to be sold at auction in another week. I talked to Lawrence that evening.

"Dear, I think I need to go back to the farm," I stated matter-of-factly as we sat at my small kitchen table eating supper.

"What? Why? You've been doing so much better since you have been away from there." He dropped his fork on his plate in surprise, making a clatter.

"I have some unfinished business." I proceeded to tell him about the encounter with Matilda and reminded him of when he, Celeste, and I had first seen the lock. "I'd like to see if we can break the curse by destroying the lock," I finished. "I feel like I owe it to her to try."

Lawrence's eyes lit up. "I think I have an idea. The place is empty now, right?"

Celeste was going through treatments now but also wanted to be involved. It was the 4th of July. We all decided that we should spend one last 4th on the farm.

Lawrence, my mom, Waylon, and I drove to the farm together. Celeste's vehicle was already there when we got there. She sat on the rear bumper of her vehicle, staring at the tree grove.

We all hugged. We shot fireworks until past midnight while reminiscing about the good times and even the bad. The place felt... sad. There was no sign of the farmer or his wife. After sitting empty for a bit, the place looked similar to what it had the first time I had seen it. For a moment, it made me miss Dakota and the way we once were.

I looked over at Celeste. She nodded towards the house. I knew where the spare key to the house was hidden and decided to try it. To my surprise, the door opened. The electricity was still on as well.

Celeste followed me in. "I thought we could walk through the house one more time," she said quietly, placing her hand on my back.

I looked back at my best friend, a sad look crossing my face. We walked silently through each empty room. The once warm, loving home we had worked so hard to fix felt cold and lonely. The smells of home cooking and clean rooms have now been replaced by a stale, unlived-in smell.

Everything felt heavy. Anguish filled my heart. A tear slipped down my face. As we came back down the stairs, I stopped. The emotions became too much. I faced the wall and slammed my fist against it as hard as I could, tears now flowing freely. "Why would I think I could help Matilda when I couldn't even save my own marriage or save this place?" I cried.

"It wasn't your fault," Celeste said. She was immediately beside me, rubbing my back as I let go of all the pain that had been building.

She let me cry until I couldn't cry anymore. Now, I was ready to do what needed to be done. Mom and Waylon had decided to go home, leaving Lawrence waiting outside for us. I took one last look at what had been my beloved home, shut off the lights, and locked the door one final time.

Celeste and I joined Lawrence by the tree grove. He held a .45 pistol in his right hand. Celeste had a flashlight. We walked to where we remembered seeing the lock for the first time, and Celeste started shining the flashlight around in the trees, looking for the lock.

After a short search, a glint amongst the branches caught our eyes. It was the lock. Lawrence took aim with the pistol but missed. He repeated the action a second time with the same result. The third time, he took his time aiming at the lock. I watched as he took a deep breath, inhaling sharply, then slowly breathing out as he squeezed the trigger.

This time, the bullet hit its target. A loud bang from the impact sounded louder than any of the fireworks we had previously been shooting. A flash of light illuminated the entire area as if it were daylight, not after midnight. The lock shattered. As it did, both Cecil and Matilda appeared out of nowhere.

Matilda appeared to transform from dirty and battered to young and beautiful. Slowly, she smiled and waved as she levitated skyward in a beam of light, then disappeared as quickly as she had appeared.

Quite to the contrary, Cecil appeared to age and become uglier. Then the earth below him appeared to open and swallow him, screaming soundlessly and grabbing to try to save himself, to no avail.

As quickly as the scene had unfolded, it was over. I stood staring at the tree where the lock had been, my boyfriend still holding the gun and my best friend beside me.

"Did you guys see that, or was it just me?" I asked. They both nodded their heads in shock. That was the last I saw of Matilda or Cecil.

The END

Epilogue

Solange: And then it was gone. I felt the first blow of the backhoe against the house as if it had hit me directly in the chest. The new owners of the farm had decided to destroy the old farmhouse after living in it during the construction of their new house. I had heard about it from the neighbor and decided to watch from a distance for closure.

I stood across the gravel road from the place, leaning against my pickup. Lawrence held my hand, and Celeste, now in remission, stood on my other side. Dakota, who now had a new girlfriend of his own and was slowly returning to the man I had once known, was there as well.

A piece of history that had withstood weather, human abuse, and the winds of time-blowing change through the country was breathing its last breath.

Just like that, years of good and bad memories were erased. Many families' lives had been seen through the windows of that old house.

Now, it is gone…

It was the end of many dreams, but hopefully, it could be the beginning of a whole new dream for everyone involved.